THE
COMING
TRIUMPH
OF THE
FREE
WORLD

Also Available in Norton Paperback Fiction

THE COMING TRIUMPH OF THE FREE WORLD

Stories by
RICK DeMARINIS

W. W. NORTON & COMPANY
New York   London

Some of the stories in this collection first appeared in periodicals, as follows: "disneyland" in *Antaeus;* "The Coming Triumph of the Free World" under the title "Rick DeMarinis to Q" in *The Quarterly;* "The Swimmer in Hard Light" under the title "The Swimmer" in *The Malahat Review;* "The Flowers of Boredom" in *The Antioch Review;* "Pagans" and "Mole" in *Harper's;* "Queen" under the title "Tenderloin" in *Colorado State Review;* and "Medicine Man" in *The Atlantic.*

Library of Congress Cataloging-in-Publication Data

DeMarinis, Rick, 1934–
The coming triumph of the free world : stories / by Rick
DeMarinis.
p.   cm.
I. Title.
PS3554.E4554C6   1991
813'.54—dc20   91-1995

ISBN 0-393-30746-8 (paper)

W. W. Norton & Company, Inc.
500 Fifth Avenue, New York, N.Y. 10110
W. W. Norton & Company, Ltd.
10 Coptic Street, London WC1A 1PU

1 2 3 4 5 6 7 8 9 0

"Of course, you may be too much of a fool to go wrong—too dull even to know you are being assaulted by the powers of darkness."

—Joseph Conrad, *Heart of Darkness*

Contents

THE
COMING
TRIUMPH
OF THE
FREE
WORLD

The Handgun

*E*very morning at 3 a.m. a dog would sit in front of our house and bark. It was a big dog, a wolfhound of some kind—Irish or Russian—and its bark broke into our sleep like a shout from God. More than loud, it was eerie. The barks came up from the street with an urgency meant to induce panic. The Huns were at the gate, the tidal wave was almost here, the volcano was about to blow. Every night I fell out of bed in a running crouch, my heart looking for a way out of its cage.

Then I'd get back into bed and pull the pillow over my head. But Raquel, stiff with rage, wouldn't let me have this easy escape. She would sit up in bed, turn on the weak lamp, and light a cigarette. "I am losing my mind," she said. "How can you expect me to go to work every morning without sleep?"

Finally, after the tenth night of the punctual dog, Raquel said, "I want you to buy a gun."

Her face was a spooky, hovering oval in the lamp's yellow glow. Her eyes were fixed on a resolute vision. I'd seen her pass through some alarming changes since I had lost my job and she had become chief breadwinner, but this tightly focused rage made me believe significant trouble was on the way.

"We can't afford a gun," I said. Which was true. We were barely making our house payments on her secretarial wages. "Not a good gun, anyway. A good rifle with a scope runs four or five hundred."

"My hunter," she said, a sneer curling her lips. "I am not talking about a rifle. I want you to get a pistol. Just a .22 target pistol. They sell them even in drugstores."

I knew it would grate on her but I tried a patronizing chuckle anyway, hoping to deflect her anger to me and thereby leave this gun business far behind. "You can't go out on the street and shoot animals. This is a neighborhood. People will get upset."

She turned to me—mechanically, I thought. Her smile would have done credit to the Borgia family. The warmth of the bed was dissipating noticeably. "I thought of that," she said. "But it's almost the Fourth of July. The neighbors will think it's only boys who could not wait to blow up their firecrackers. No one will get out of bed to investigate."

"You've been thinking about this for some time," I observed, mostly to myself.

"Yes. I have. And we won't go into the street. We will shoot from the window, behind the curtains. We will put Kleenex over the barrel so that the flash will not be seen."

"You'd be murdering someone's companion, a pet . . ."

She gave me a lingering, abstracted look, the look she might give a complete stranger who had offered a demented opinion. "You," she said, "suffocate me."

The distance between us enlarged. Madness does that. It seemed like a trend. Her response to straightforward remarks might come from left field or from outside the park. I thought she might be in the early stages of a breakdown. The thought depressed me. I got up and went into the bathroom, where I took an Elavil.

I didn't want a gun in the house. I'd recently read a sobering statistic: of all handgun deaths in private homes, only a tiny percentage involved intruders. The majority of victims were members of the gun owner's immediate family. The usual motive was suicide. And sometimes, but not rarely, murder *and* suicide. I thought: *Baloney.* Then I saw that it made perfect sense. I couldn't count the number of times I'd raised my finger to my head and said "Bang" after reading, say, a turn-off notice from the Power Company, or a credit-threatening letter from Penney's or Sears. A finger to the temple and the sadly muttered "Bang" is a clown's gesture, wistful at best, but signifying the ever-present wish to put out one's lights.

"Go to Mel's Pawnshop tomorrow," Raquel, or the person Raquel was in the process of becoming, said when I came back to the bedroom. "They sell fine guns there for under one hundred dollars."

She'd turned out the lamp and was sitting naked next to the window, looking down on the dog. It had quit barking and was just staring, like a rejected lover, at the cold beauty of Raquel's unforgiving silhouette.

"It's against the *law* to shoot fine guns in the city," I said, mocking her lambent Hispanic fire and lilt. "It's a felony."

"I am not interested in your *putrefacto* laws," she said.

"What do you know about Mel's Pawnshop, anyway?" I said. I stepped behind her and put my hands on her moon-dusty shoulders. The moon was nearly full and she was incandescent with a chalky light. Given the state of our lives, 3 a.m. sex was unlikely, but this crazy moonlit woman in the window broke the spell hard times puts on flesh. I slipped my hands down to her breasts like a repossessor.

She hunched away from me. "I want to put a bullet in that dog's throat," she said.

I went back to bed as the dog resumed its pointless assault on our lives. "I am not going to Mel's," I said.

"Fine, St. Francis," she said. "I'll go."

But she didn't go. She was afraid to. The pawnshop area of town was full of aimless psychotics. Now and then one of them would be picked up for a crime committed in another part of the state or country. In fact, a serial murderer had been arrested in Mel's a year ago as he was trying to trade a necklace made of human kneecaps for a machete.

The next night a weather front moved in and the air was stifling. The changed atmospherics improved the acoustics of the neighborhood. The dog, it seemed, was in bed with us.

"I can't stand it!" Raquel screamed. "You have to do something!" She pulled the pillow off my head and threw it across the bedroom.

I got up and opened the window. "Shut up, dog!" I yelled, but I might as well have been arguing with a magpie. We were not on the same wavelength. The odd timbre of the dog's bark gave it an almost human quality. I could nearly make myself believe I was hearing a kind of garbled English. "What what *what?*" or "Hot, hot, what?" But there was also a forlorn tone that was not translatable. A canine refusal to accept some wrenching loss. I went back to bed.

"I've got this feeling, hon," I said. "Like that dog is in mourning for its lost mate." We'd called the Animal Control Cop days ago and his white van toured the neighborhood, picking up strays. Maybe the big dog lost his ladylove in that sweep.

Raquel turned on the bed lamp and studied my face for signs of mockery or perhaps derangement. "Are you *crazy?*" she asked. "Dogs don't mate for life like *swans*. They screw any bitch in heat. Don't try to turn that monster into a brokenhearted family man."

Then she said the thing that forced the issue. "Look, *hon*," she mocked. "Either you get that gun or I am going to find somewhere else to sleep at night."

My joblessness, and now my refusal to take action in an emergency, had turned her against me. "All right," I said. "I'll get the gun."

The next day, after I had made breakfast and Raquel had gone to work, I walked through the neighborhood looking for the dog. I'd already done this several times, but now I knocked on doors and asked questions. No one would admit to owning such a dog, not on our street or on the several adjacent streets. But even more curious than this, no one admitted to having heard the dog bark. Evidently its tirades were sharply directional, like the beam from a radar antenna, hitting only the thing it aimed at.

"Did you get it?" Raquel asked me when she got home from work.

I stalled. "Bindle-stiff chicken tonight, darling," I said. "Plus asparagus à la Milwaukee vinaigrette." These were recipes I had invented. I was proud of them. They were Raquel's favorites.

"You didn't get it," she said.

"All Mel had were big-caliber revolvers—.357s and .44s. Nothing we could use comfortably. We'd wreck the neighborhood with those cannons."

"You didn't go," she said.

I stuttered, a dead giveaway, then faced a wall of spiting silence the rest of the evening. She didn't touch my wonderful dinner.

The following morning at nine-thirty I saw Dr. Selbiades, my shrink. I told him all about the dog, the gun, and Raquel's threat. I had not called him up about this crisis, and I could tell that it miffed him a bit.

"So," he said, in that loftily humble, arrogant, self-effacing way of his. "Your wife wants you to get a . . . *gun*."

Selbiades is not a Freudian, so this was only a joke—meant, no doubt, to get even with me for keeping secrets.

"I've decided to get one this afternoon."

"Just like that?" he said, rocking back in his five-hundred-dollar leather-covered swivel chair.

"Yes. A .22 automatic."

"It would be a mistake, my friend," he said.

"Probably. But I don't see that I have a choice."

He stood up and flexed his hairy arms over his head and yawned. His yawn was as healthy and as uninhibited as a lion's. He scratched his ribs vigorously, then sat down again. He was wearing a T-shirt and Levi's and running shoes. He never wore anything else, at least in his office. "Christ, man," he said at last, his thick neck corded, it seemed, with redundant veins and arteries. "Of course you have a choice! Unless . . ."

I bit. "Unless?"

"Unless you hate her."

"*Hate* her? I love her! What do you mean, *hate?*"

"It just sounds like some classic passive-aggressive bullshit, my friend. You're giving her enough rope to hang herself with."

"I am terrified of losing her," I said, my voice ragged.

Selbiades swiveled his chair around abruptly, so that he now faced the window behind his desk. "There is, of course, a level on which what you say is true," he said, his tone suggesting a far too intimate knowledge of mankind. His window gave out on a view of fields, freshly scraped down to naked earth in preparation for a town-house development called Vista Buena Bonanza. He clasped his hairy hands behind his head and contemplated this field. He owned it and was a partner in the new development. I envied him: he was the happiest man I knew.

"What about bullets?" Raquel asked that evening. I gave her the small paper bag that had four boxes of .22 ammo in it. She snatched the bag from me and inspected each box.

"No blanks," I said, thinking that blanks would have been fine. I was sure all she wanted to do was scare the dog off, not actually wound it.

She looked haggard sitting at the kitchen table, holding the pistol in one hand and sorting through bullets with the other. Then she put the gun and bullets in one messy pile and shoved them to the center of the table. She stood up and hugged me. "I am so proud of you at this moment," she said.

But it was a soldierly embrace. French or Russian, it would have involved tight-lipped kisses on both cheeks. A distinct warpage had entered our lives.

While I did a stir-fry, she paced around the kitchen smoking cigarettes, lost in strategy. She had been putting on weight and her heavy stride made the wok shimmy. I guessed that she'd put on twenty or thirty pounds since she'd taken the job at the courthouse. I hated to see that. In spite of our quick lip service to the contrary, physical attraction is the first thing that draws men to women, and vice versa. Time and mileage do their damage, but Raquel was too young to lose her figure. She had the long-muscled legs of a Zulu princess, along with the high-rising arch of spirited buttocks. Her torso was wide and ribby, the breasts not large but dominant and forthright. But now that rare geometry had been put in danger by the endless goodies office workers have to contend with every day. The county office in which she processed words seemed more like a giant deli than an arm of government. Often she would bring me pastries oozing lemon curd or brandied compote, or giant sandwiches on Kaiser buns thick with ham or beef, and on special occasions such as office parties, entire boxes of sour cream chocolate cookies, brownies, or Bismarcks. She wouldn't step on the scale. When I suggested it she snapped, "I know, I know, I've put on a couple of pounds. I don't need to have it shoved in my face."

But it was more than her waistline that was changing. She began to embrace opinions that seemed alien to her nature. She'd sit on the sofa in front of the evening news with watchdog attentiveness. ("See how Rather works in the knee-jerk liberal point of view?" "Look at the expression on Brokaw's face when he mentions the Contras. Looks like he wants to spit.") In the past she had no coherent politics. She was resolutely apolitical, in fact. But now she was listing sharply to the no-nonsense Right.

"The people are going to take law and order into their own hands if the courts keep turning loose the rapists and killers," she once said.

"That's how a society destroys itself," I suggested, fatuously, I admit.

Raquel scoffed. It was the first time in our eight-year marriage that she had shown outright contempt for me. It stung. The scar is still warm. "That is how a society *saves* itself," she said.

And, on another occasion, she said that the bureaucrats didn't care a bit about the common man. "All they care about is raising taxes so they can keep their soft jobs." She had good evidence for this, having spent the last six months working for the Department of Streets.

That first night of the gun was electric with adrenaline. We couldn't sleep at all. We watched TV until 2 a.m., then went up to the bedroom. We got undressed—no pajamas or nightgown, as it was another hot, humid night—and got in bed. Raquel was giddy with high excitement. I was tense, and not looking forward to the dog's appointed hour. I wished now that my passive-aggressive bullshit had not expressed itself so classically.

The bed got swampy with body steam. Raquel threw off the sheet and thin blanket and sat up. She took the gun off the night table and couched it on her belly. Goosebumps, triggered by the cold steel, radiated upward to her breasts, stiffening the nipples, and downward to her thighs, making them twitch. The moon was on the wane but still bright. A thin film of sweat made her body glow metallic. *Oh rarest of metals!* I thought, choking back a desperate love. The gun muzzle slipped down into the dark delta at the vertex of her thighs. Perversions of wild variety and orientation presented themselves to me.

"Forget it," Raquel said, sensing my state of mind. "He might start any minute now."

"It's not three yet. It's only two-thirty."

I was pleading. I hated myself, a beggar in my own bed.

"Afterward," she said, her voice oddly abstract in the abstract light of the moon. "It will be *better* afterward."

I couldn't see her eyes, just the black skull-holes that held them. She was smiling.

I snapped on the bed lamp, but didn't look at her. I wanted to avoid her, to organize my thoughts; I wanted to hold back the clock. I picked up a *Newsweek* from the magazine rack under the night table and flipped it open. I read about a woman in Pennsylvania who boiled her baby and sent the parts of the cooked body to a newspaper editor who had denounced abortion. Another article suggested that eighty percent of all children under the age of twelve will one day be the victims of a violent crime. I switched to the opinion columns, but those genteel, sharp-witted souls seemed to be writing about a world in which sanity was a possibility.

Then it was three o'clock. "How do you shoot this thing?" Raquel asked, looking at the gun as if for the first time.

"You aim and pull the trigger. It's easy," I said. I heard my passive-aggressive bullshit sprocketing these words out of my lungs.

"Isn't there something here called the safety?" she asked. It made me happy that the enormity of the coming violence had made her a bit timid.

"That little lever, up on the handle, I think." Actually my knowledge of guns was not much better than hers.

"*Where?*"

"Push it up, or maybe down. I don't know."

The gun, wobbling around in her hand, gradually aimed itself at her throat as she fiddled with its levers and knobs.

"Jesus Christ!" I said, grabbing the gun away from her. It went off. It shot a Currier and Ives print off the wall. It was an original, given to me by my grandmother. *Fast Trotters in Harlem Lane, N.Y.* Men in silk hats driving fine teams of horses down the dirt roads of nineteenth-century Harlem.

Raquel burst into tears. It shocked me. Not the tears but the realization that I could not remember the last time she had cried. I put my arms around her, half expecting her to shove me away. She didn't.

Then something else happened. Or failed to happen. It was three-fifteen and there was no dog in the street calling to us. "Listen, honey," I said.

But her sobs had been on hold too long to be put off. She cried for another five minutes. Then I said it again, as gently as I could. "Listen, Raquel. No *dog*."

We both went to the window. The street was empty. Whatever the big dog had wanted to get off his chest was gone. He had exorcised himself, or at least that's what I hoped. There was the possibility that he'd taken a night off and would come back. But I didn't have to think about that now. Thinking about that, and what I would have to do about it, could wait.

I went downstairs and made a pot of hot chocolate. I brought two big mugs of it back to the bedroom. But Raquel was already asleep. I was too rattled to sleep. I went back down and drank hot chocolate until 5 a.m. The dog never showed up.

When I went back upstairs, the sun was flooding the bedroom with its good-hearted light. It was the same good-hearted light that fell on the heads of baby boilers and saints alike, unconditionally.

The last thing I saw before dropping off to sleep that morning was the gun, shining on the night table like a blue wish. I had one of those half-waking dreams that give you the feeling that you've understood something. I understood that the barking dog had been a sponsor for the gun. The gun had sought us out, and found us, with the assistance of the dog. *Go to sleep, you fool,* Raquel said. But that was the dream, too, and I realized that the gun had summoned, again with the aid of the dog, real changes in Raquel.

Morning dreams always wake me up, insisting that I register their fake significance. I got out of bed and went to the bathroom.

I took a long look at my face. It had more mileage on it than my life justified. I rummaged through the stock of pills in the medicine cabinet, then went back to bed armed with Seconal against smart-ass dreams. The gun caught my eye again. It had a tight, self-satisfied sheen, like a deceptively well-groomed relative from a disgraced branch of the family who'd come to claim a permanent place in our home.

disneyland

Pixel. A small word, filling a few bytes of memory at most, but it sat in Albert Court's mind like a huge bird of prey. No other words could get past *pixel.* He was blocked again. The brain could store millions of megabytes of information, and yet here was *pixel* in ten-foot-high neon letters declaring itself supreme, the only word in the world.

Albert looked at his damaged son, trying to force the stopper out of his mind, hoping for simple fluency. "Tommy," he said, but the obstinate *pixel* shoved the next word aside.

Tommy Court regarded his sweating father. *My sire,* he thought, amused.

Albert touched his son's lips with a Kleenex. The sedative, tranquilizer, antidepressant, or whatever it was they'd given him caused the boy to salivate heavily. Tommy turned away, refusing his father's attentions.

Then, mercifully, *pixel* opened its wings and sailed out of Albert's mind. Wiping his forehead with another Kleenex, he said, cheerful with relief, "Well, Tomaso, isn't this one grade-A hell of a fix?" He laughed, jovial at the sudden release of language.

Tommy was being kept in the hospital for psychiatric observation because of what he'd done to himself. The family physician, Dr. Bud Rossetti, thought it best. It wasn't a private room—Albert's Health Maintenance Organization didn't permit private rooms—and the fat man in the other bed flooded the small room with the steady rasp of difficult breathing. The man was sitting up in bed, bent over a crossword puzzle. "What's a four-letter word for 'think tank'?" he asked.

"Rand," Tommy said, holding his bandaged arms over his head, like a referee's signal for "touchdown."

"Come again?" the fat man said, staring dubiously at Tommy over his half-moon reading glasses.

"Rand," Tommy repeated. "The Rand Corporation."

"Oh, Christ. Of course." The fat man leaned into his puzzle, wheezing.

"Tommy," Albert said, his voice hushed discreetly. "Sylvia's a wreck. Look, you're her only child. You know how she feels about you. What you've done to her . . . No, scratch that, Tomaso. I meant, what happened—" He stopped himself, realizing too late his blunder.

Tommy wouldn't let his father off the hook. *"Go for it, Pops. Say it."*

"No, son. You know that's not what I meant to say."

"Sure it was. You wanted to say that what I did to myself was actually meant for puddly old Sylvia's benefit. Every fucking thing that sends her up the walls is old Tomaso's fault, like she had a full deck before I started screwing up my life. Right?"

Albert glanced nervously at the fat man, but the fat man was engrossed in his puzzle, or at least was civil enough to be faking it. "Seven letters," he murmured to himself, "meaning 'danger for the unwary.' "

Albert picked up the water pitcher and filled the glass on Tommy's night table. He drank all of the water, then refilled the glass.

Wriggle, wriggle, Tommy thought, smiling faintly.

Words: in the best of times they were difficult for Albert. They were nearly impossible when he had to deal with crisis situations. Sometimes he believed he was dysphasic, and at other, more despairing moments, he thought he had a form of Parkinson's disease, a radical decay of the area of the brain responsible for speech.

He had to dredge for words, even when the stakes were light, and the dredging made him sweat. And yet he was a crack salesman for Funtron, Inc., a manufacturer of recreational software for personal computers. His colleagues on the sales team decided that this simple incongruity was responsible for Albert's success. People in the trade, they reasoned, were probably fed up with the slick, hotshot, silver-tongued types that dominated the early years of the business. They no doubt found a quiet man's struggle for words downright refreshing, even *touching*. The theory was hard to believe, but no one could advance a second explanation.

Tommy swung his pajamaed legs out of the bed and walked around the fat man's bed to the room's single window. A work crew was demolishing an old building across from the hospital. There was a message scrawled in spray paint on the remaining upright wall of the old building: HANG UP THE PIN, WILMA. The building was an old flophouse, the city's last blemish. The old flophouse had been a refuge for winos and homeless psychotics. A city councilman had announced, "We intend to enter the twenty-first century with a clean slate. These reminders of defeat and degradation must be erased from the public memory."

Tommy thought: *I'll get on the pin, like pissy old Wilma, heavy into scag. I'll get totaled on smack, crack, and what-you-got-Jack. I will free-base among the kamikaze zombies and go down in flames.*

When Tommy came back to his bed, Albert said, "Motherboard." The new stopper had waddled into his mind unnoticed and tricked him into verbalizing it. And now it sat, wide and sleek as a hippo or beached whale, jamming up the little speech Albert had prepared to defuse the situation. Sweat rolled down from his hairline into his eyebrows and down his cheeks. He drank more water, praying wordlessly for release.

"I don't think we're on the same page, Pop," Tommy said.

"*Pit*fall," the fat man said, triumphant.

Albert drove home. His wife, Sylvia, was under sedation. A nurse was in the house, sent over, he guessed, by Dr. Rossetti. Albert hadn't asked for a nurse, but was relieved to find a trained professional there. It was a good idea, although he wasn't sure his HMO would pay for it. No matter, he'd had an excellent year. Funtron, Inc., had come up with six innovative games, interactive fictions, and all of them were hot sellers. *Gaslight,* a Victorian romance, had stunned the industry with its success. Twelve retail outlets in his territory had the software on back order. No one thought *Gaslight* would become a mainstay of the Funtron line, but the public, so far at least, couldn't get enough of it. Letters from ecstatic customers came in daily. They loved how the program allowed Jack the Ripper a wide range of character traits, from remorseless, deadpan sadism to the engaging wit of a Lothario. They loved how they could program Prince Edward, Lloyd George, and young Winston Churchill to become players in labyrinthine love affairs that were consummated in the most glamorous cities in Europe.

The nurse was sitting on the sofa watching a soap opera. Albert stepped in front of the TV set. "How is she?" he asked.

The nurse, after trying to look past Albert's legs, said, irritably, "You know. Breathing in then breathing out. Would you scoot over, please? I think Inez is getting ready to give in to that bastard Ronnie Powers."

"Is she . . . can I see her?" he asked.

"Up to you. She's sort of asleep, though."

Albert went into the kitchen and opened the fridge. He wasn't hungry, but knew he hadn't eaten since Tommy tried to kill himself. He took out some sliced cheese, pastrami, the pickles, mayonnaise, and a can of Diet Sprite. He made a sandwich and carried it into the living room. He sat in his recliner and watched the soap opera. A woman—Inez, he imagined—was trying to light a cigarette while lying across a bed. She was wearing black bikini panties and bra. "Damn you," she said to her lighter, as the scene dissolved to a man crouched in a stairwell.

Albert glanced at the nurse. She was young and exotic-looking. Possibly Asian. Possibly Martian. She had smooth amber skin and streaked, triple-toned hair. Her name tag said LEEANN. Her hair was auburn, yellow, and black. It furled tightly out from her head like a frozen banner. She looked competent. She had a beautiful figure under a crisp, light-blue uniform.

"Go for a sandwich?" Albert said, holding up the remains of his.

The nurse held up her hand to quiet him. "Wait," she said.

"Here it comes. This really gives me the blues. I wish she'd kick that jerkoff Ronnie Powers out."

Inez had given up trying to light her cigarette. She was face down on the bed now, sobbing. Ronnie Powers, a dark, wavy-haired man, sneered at Inez from a doorway. He threw some money on the floor. "You're trash," he said. "You'll always be trash."

The nurse lit a cigarette and blew smoke at the TV set. "I *mean*," she said, rolling her eyes dramatically, "this Ronnie Powers guy is *such* a dick."

Albert went upstairs. Sylvia was curled up under the electric blanket. Her face had the transparent look of white wax. The room smelled of wet eucalyptus leaves. Albert sat down on the bed. Sylvia didn't open her eyes or change position but reached out for him very slowly and sought his hand. He took her hand and kissed it, then squeezed it tightly. "Old Tomaso," he said, his voice hoarse. "He's going to be okay."

Sylvia's eyes fluttered, then opened. They looked dreamy and carefree. Except for her color and the stringy condition of her hair, Albert could almost believe she was well.

"It's true, darling. You should see him. Oh, he's mad as hell . . . at him*self* . . . for doing such a thing. But that's understandable. He's quite a Tomaso, that kid."

Sylvia gradually brought her husband into focus. Then she frowned. "Why?" she said.

Rows of modems tractored through his mind. He took a deep breath. *Modem, modem,* like heartbeats, scattered his thoughts. He shrugged. "Girl," he finally managed. "Fickle girl . . ." He felt dizzy; a roaring in his ears made him steady himself on the bed.

His wife looked away. The lids of her eyes were thick as crepe. "Girl," she murmured, her drug-swollen tongue unable to flex properly around the syllable.

Albert patted her hand.

"What's wrong with you?" his wife said, her voice suddenly alert.

Albert's heart knocked against his ribs. "What? Me? Nothing."

He hesitated. "I feel sort of . . . unplugged from my database," he said, chuckling nervously.

"You sound—" she began, but the drug asserted itself again and the thought dwindled away until it became the sound of her own breath as it labored through her nostrils.

Dr. Rossetti had culled the story from Tommy. Then, in the privacy of his office, he told it to Albert, not sparing the details. The girl, Barbara Sunderlin, had decided that she needed a more educational range of experience. She and Tommy had been going steady, but she felt that their relationship was becoming too confining and that it would ultimately be a sounder relationship if it were more "open." Besides, she was a freshman at State College and he was a senior in high school. She was not especially pretty, but she had no trouble in getting other dates. She told Tommy about them. When things went badly for her, she'd cry on Tommy's shoulder and tell him what had happened in vivid detail. She told Tommy that she needed him, that he was the strong, silent, clean-cut type. Some of those fraternity boys were degenerate beasts, she said. They were soulless harbingers of a mechanistic future. Tommy was a refreshing throwback, without the pregenital neuroses that characterized the perverts she was seeing regularly now. It is beyond your imagination, Tommy, she told him, what those fraternity boys make me do. Dr. Rossetti had tried to put this part of the story into clinical terms, but, even so, Albert was still embarrassed at the anatomy of the sexual imagination.

Tommy had raged. He was a strong boy, a weight lifter and member of the high school wrestling team. He wanted to twist the heads off those fraternity creeps, he said. But Barbara wouldn't give him the name of the fraternity. It was for his sake, she said, that the name must be kept secret. She would blame herself if something happened. She told him she loved him and would always love him. He believed her. He told her he would always love her, too. They exchanged rings. These rings symbolize the eternal, *spiritual* nature of our relationship, she said. Our love is sane and simple and shall always remain so, she said. You are my sunny knight in bright armor, Tommy, you are my clean ray of optimism and decency in a toxic-waste-dump world. Tommy wanted to go steady again, even get engaged, but Barbara said she intended to become a serious poet and needed the kind of wide-spectrum experience she was now beginning to acquire. I must descend into the mire, she said. I am an erotic explorer entering the dark jungles of desire. I intend to encounter the beasts who live in that jungle and thus, step by step, gain an understanding of the human animal himself. It's the only way. Academic psychologists, even clinical therapists, do not have access to the beast on an eye-to-eye basis. They remain antiseptically aloof.

But Tommy couldn't accept her behavior. Her exploration of the dark jungles of desire distressed him. The types of things she was doing with the fraternity boys were absolutely beyond belief. He insisted she stop. It isn't possible for me to stop, she said. Don't be a child, Tommy, she said. Try to grasp the elemental nature of my quest. On one occasion, Tommy, in a tearful rage, slapped her face.

Their relationship began to change. Barbara became abusive. She began to ridicule his naïveté. She sent him a poem that pointed out his self-delusions. Finally, she sent him a collection of Polaroids of herself and several others. That night, after drinking a pint of vodka, Tommy hacked at his wrists and arms. The cuts were serious but the main arteries were not involved.

Albert had called Barbara's father. His rage and embarrassment flooded his mind with thought-blocking nonsense words. Mr. Sunderlin was mystified by the call. He had no idea what his daughter and Albert's son had been up to. He was a pleasant, soft-spoken man, a civil engineer with the county. Albert was able, eventually, to give the man a few clues, and the man filled the awkward silence with some platitudes about the generation gap. He recommended a book called *How to Deal Effectively with Your Problem Teen.* Albert choked out the word *microstuffer,* and another long silence ensued. Then, when the stopper drifted out of his mind, he said, quickly, "My son tried to take his own life."

"Oh, good Lord," said Mr. Sunderlin. "I had no idea."

The nurse, LeeAnn, went to the guest room after *Dynasty*. She came out a few minutes later in a bathrobe. There was a flowery shower cap on her head and a transparent gel on her face. "You can call me if she wants something," she told Albert.

She seemed friendlier now. Her robe was partially open, and her fine, tawny skin gleamed between her breasts. Albert started to say something, but she smiled and put her finger to her lips.

"I sleep real light," she said, "don't worry."

Albert watched TV for a while but the jokes on the Letterman show were exceptionally snide and the response from the audience seemed eagerly cruel. Albert switched off the set and went out into the garage. He had a fully equipped workshop there. Against one wall were several woodworking machines, but he had never really used any of them. Sylvia and Tommy had surprised him a few Christmases ago with a complete Home Craftsman set. Albert often complained about not having a hobby, something to do with his hands. His work at Funtron was mainly mental. He ran on nervous, caffeine-enhanced energy and was exhausted most of the time. A workshop with good tools seemed just the thing. But he never got around to learning how to use them. He'd gotten as far as buying some quality pine and alder, but had only cut some boards up to see how the saws worked. He liked the sound of the saws. He liked the deep thrum of the strong electrical motors, and the whine of the spinning blades made him feel relaxed. His mind, filled with the whine and thrum of the machinery, would be cleared of its useless clutter.

He turned on the table saw and sat on his stool. The table saw had the most satisfying sound of all the tools. Its motor was the largest, and the big, savage-looking blade made a breathy whir. He went back into the kitchen and fixed himself a large Scotch and soda, then returned to the garage and the moving saw. He stayed there an hour, nothing in his mind but a ten-inch circle of steel with razor-sharp teeth spinning at thousands of RPMs.

He carried another drink to Tommy's room. He sat on the bed and looked at the elaborately decorated walls. Pennants, comical signs (CLOSE TOILET BEFORE FLUSHING. NO PEDDLERS. BEWARE OF VICIOUS TURTLE. SPEED BUMPS). There were posters of rock stars— all with the same annoying expression on their pocked, ghost-white faces.

He turned on Tommy's Apple II-e and was surprised to see that he had *Gaslight* already loaded in. Albert touched a key and a question appeared on the screen: "Who is Jack the Ripper?" Albert, feeling a little drunk, typed "I am," but the program wouldn't accept that response. It scolded him and asked that he answer the question within "game parameters." Albert switched the machine off.

He looked at Tommy's barbell shoved up against the closet door. He went over to it and set his drink down on the floor. He gripped the weight with both hands and tried to lift it. The barbell didn't move. He picked up his drink and sipped at it. Then he saw the poems. They were on Tommy's desk, next to the Apple, under a half-eaten doughnut. He knew they were poems because the words were scattered on the pages. Each poem was signed by Barbara Sunderlin. The signature was large and childishly elaborate.

This is not prying, he told himself. The poems were out in the open. Removing a doughnut doesn't count. He slid a poem out from the stack and read it:

> *my bittersweet rose*
> > *burns*
> *with a fire*
> > *of tongues*

He took another poem from deeper in the stack:

> *night thoughts of bulls*
> *thunder*
> > *in my field*
> *O how I moo*
> > *at the boney moon*

The next poem was no poem at all:

> *in it*
> *in it*
> *in it*
> *in it*
> *in it*

There was a poem called "Quixote in Blue Denim." It was dedicated to Tommy Court:

> *Grab your section*
> *Sunny Jim, while*
> *I tell you a tale*
> *Of animal connection*

Albert was unable to read the rest.

He sat in his car for several minutes in front of the Sunderlin home, thinking. He had to have better reasons for coming here than curiosity and anger. But nothing else occurred to him. He went to the door, poems in hand. A woman answered. She was a tall, striking blonde, elegantly dressed. The Sunderlins were evidently going out for the evening. This immediately threw his planned speech into a disarray of broken phrases. He felt foolish. The woman was smoking a long cigarette.

"Albert Court," he said, at last.

The woman raised a penciled eyebrow and blew a thread of smoke out one side of her mouth. "Oh, of course," she said. "You're the boy's father."

Mr. Sunderlin, wearing a chocolate-brown tux, stepped up behind his wife. "Come in, Mr. Court," he said, sliding back his sleeve to glance at his watch. "We have a few minutes."

Barbara Sunderlin was sitting in a high-back chair reading a thin volume of poetry.

"Babsie, honey," Mr. Sunderlin said. "Mr. Court is here."

The girl looked up from her book. She was wearing glasses. The lenses were narrow rectangles, smoke-tinted. She looked over them at Albert with a flat, analytical gaze. She was not attractive. She had a high, round forehead and she wore her hair swept back into an old-fashioned bun. Her nose was long and thin, the nostrils pinched asthmatically. Her lips were dark and full and frozen in a pout. Albert could not believe she was a nineteen-year-old girl. She looked thirty-five.

She closed her book and stood up. She was tall and slender, but her breasts were sharply conical in her dark red cardigan.

"Oh, Mr. Court!" she said, suddenly distraught. She went to him and threw her arms around his neck. She put her head on his shoulder and moaned. Albert was stunned. Her loud, wet sobs were muffled in the cloth of his jacket. He felt her thin body shuddering against him.

Albert didn't know what to do. He'd walked into this house, prepared to tell them what had happened to Tommy, whose fault it was, and to demand some sort of reparation, but now he was helpless as the sobbing girl clung to him as if he were her sole emotional support in this crisis.

He was still holding the poems. He looked over Barbara's quaking shoulder at Mr. and Mrs. Sunderlin, hoping for rescue. The Sunderlins were attractive, sophisticated people, and Albert began to lose his nerve before their stylish self-confidence. They were the kind of people he had always envied, even though they were not economically better off than he was. He raised his hands stiffly and patted Barbara on the back in a clumsy attempt to console her. The poems rattled, calling attention to themselves. Mrs. Sunderlin looked faintly amused, but her amusement faded quickly to boredom. Her perfect eyebrows were arched and she was squinting through a screen of blue smoke.

"I'm intruding," Albert said, trying to pull away from the sobbing girl. He wanted to leave now, but could not make himself utter the words that would allow him to do this without appearing a complete fool. The splendid calm of the Sunderlins had somehow canceled his right to speak to them on equal terms. The complaint he had intended to make them listen to was gone; he couldn't even recall who it had been intended for, the girl or her parents. A storm of self-hatred scattered his thoughts. He felt guilty and shy. Barbara, as if sensing his extreme discomfort, tightened her embrace. Her small sobs warmed his neck. Albert kept patting her on the back, and the rattling sheaf of poems grew perversely loud.

"So, you're into software," Mr. Sunderlin said.

"Just sales," Albert said.

"Don't knock sales. The world turns on sales. Eleanor—my wife, Eleanor—she's into real estate."

The woman's faint smile seemed to summon up a stopper. *Parser* slipped into Albert's mind, a vivid python, and began to uncoil. "Parser," he said, blushing instantly.

Mr. Sunderlin chuckled suavely. "Babsie, why don't you let the poor gentleman go? I think he under*stands* your feelings."

Barbara stepped away from Albert and leveled a vicious look at her father.

Sylvia's condition became worse. Dr. Bud Rossetti prescribed a more potent tranquilizer. "It's time to upscale the chemistry, Albert," he said. "I think it's time to move up to the phenothiazines."

Albert had mentioned Sylvia's dreams. They threw her into terrible panics. She screamed on waking. Sometimes she wasn't sure she'd been asleep. And when she was awake, she sometimes believed she was still sleeping. In one dream there had been a basket of bleeding fruit on the breakfast table. Tommy would not eat. She tried to give him a bloody apple but he turned his face away. A butterfly big as a cat sat on top of the fruit basket. It turned to her and opened its jaws. Sylvia had thought that the butterfly was trying to speak to her. She got the idea it wanted to say her name. "I couldn't," Albert said, "make her stop. Screaming, I mean."

Dr. Rossetti wrote two prescriptions in a hasty scrawl. He shook his big dark head back and forth as he wrote. "Grim city, Albert," he said. "All we can do is pray that it passes. The human organism is amazingly resilient. Think of it as weather, Albert. Good air will eventually blow the bad air out."

"No, it won't," Albert said.

Dr. Rossetti took Albert in his big arms. "You have my personal guarantee," he said.

Albert pushed the big doctor away. "Thanks," he said.

"You're a quality guy, Albert," Dr. Rossetti said.

Albert left Sylvia in the care of LeeAnn and drove out to the hospital. Tommy was having his wrists and arms rebandaged and after that a psychologist was going to give him another test. He couldn't have visitors for a couple of hours. Albert decided to spend the time in the waiting room. He didn't want to go back home, even though it was only a ten-minute drive.

"Well, hi there, Mr. Court," someone said.

Albert looked up from the copy of *Time* he'd been reading. The harsh white light of the waiting room made his eyes blur.

"It's me. It is I. You know. Barbara Sunderlin."

She had been sitting across from him, not more than twelve feet away. How long had she been there? The feeling that she had just materialized, unbeckoned, struck him. His heart tripped on the idea, then began to beat noticeably. The mind was a magic crystal: things appeared in it out of nowhere. His whole life seemed to him like a series of abrupt manifestations, things and events without antecedents. Everything discrete, self-sufficient, like the binary digits of a computer program. Nothing had the old continuity of the analog model of reality. *Multiplexor* slipped into his mind, then a quick series of flip-flops between *and-gate, or-gate,* and *zero-wait-state.*

Barbara came over and sat in the chair next to him. "Mr. Court, I can't tell you how *awful* I feel," she said, her voice rising. The receptionist looked up from her desk. "Look," Barbara said. "I was going to give this to Tommy!" She held up a small gift-wrapped package. "It's a new wallet. Alligator. A get-well present." Her voice thickened with self-loathing. Other people in the waiting room were looking at them. The receptionist frowned at Albert. "What kind of rotten *creep* would give a boy who tried to kill himself a fucking alligator *wallet?*" She began to cry.

"Maybe we should talk outside," Albert said.

They went out to the parking lot and sat in Albert's car. Barbara was now weeping uncontrollably. She put her head on Albert's chest. She didn't seem thirty-five years old to Albert now. She seemed twelve. He was grateful for the anonymity of the parking lot.

"Drive me someplace," Barbara said, lifting her face from his chest.

She was calmer now, and Albert was grateful for that. "Sure," he said. "Where do you want to go?"

"Anywhere. I always drive around whenever I feel too shitty for words."

"I'll take you home," he said.

"No. Not there. Not home."

Albert drove aimlessly for a while, allowing himself to be drawn into this lane or that turn by the random pressures of traffic. He, too, found that driving around casually was a soothing experience. It was a California thing, he decided, it's what we do. And now that the access ramps were computer-controlled, it made the whole process a lot easier.

He merged into the fast traffic on the Santa Ana freeway. Barbara was slumped against the door, the side of her face pressed against the window. Her expression was calm and vacant. She stared straight down the freeway, eyes relaxed on distance.

"Listen, Mr. Court," she said abstractedly. "I've been thinking. I've got this great idea."

"I'd better be getting home," he said.

"Beautiful," she said. "Just fucking beautiful."

They drove without speaking. To the right of the freeway, the Alps of Disneyland loomed against the grainy sky. The spires and towers of Fantasyland leaped up at them like a forgotten childhood dream returning, colossal and strange, as if it had been growing cancerously in some dark corner of the mind.

"My father is an intellectual snob," Barbara said. "You know the kind—reads Aldous Huxley and Ayn Rand, always quoting them. He never once took me to Disneyland. Even when I was in grade school and couldn't have understood what he meant, he made cutting remarks about this place. Hell, maybe he was right. I don't know. But I've always wanted to come here. It's as though there's this denied child within me, and this has been her secret ambition forever."

"*Okay,*" Albert said, flipping on his turn signal.

Albert bought two multiple-ride coupon books. The crowd was relatively small. Albert and Barbara were the only couple on the trip to the moon. There were only four other passengers on the submarine voyage. There were more people on the flatboat trip through the jungle, but it was a quiet crowd. They seemed unaware of the festive nature of the giant amusement park. Barbara called them Russians. In fact, they did look like foreigners—East Europeans, possibly Russians. The men were wearing dark, bulky suits and the women were stocky matrons in low heels. There were no children with them. It was a solemn crowd that looked somehow displaced, and the entire trip through the jungle seemed more like a forced trek to some grim place of exile than an amusement. The crowd at the Haunted House, to Albert's relief, seemed more typical.

"I just *love* it," Barbara said gaily. "Don't you, Mr. Court?" They were out on a mall, strolling among human-sized mice.

He wanted to answer her, he wanted to say, Yes, I love it, but he frowned and looked at his watch instead. "Almost four," he said.

A very tall man wearing only Jockey shorts stepped into their path. He'd been hiding behind a closed information kiosk. "Nay!" he shouted. He was at least six feet ten inches tall and his coarse gray hair fell past his shoulders, stiff with grime. Black hearts the size of dimes were tattooed across his chest. Little red arrows, the tips dripping blood, pierced the black hearts. "Nay!" he repeated, his voice cracking with either emotion or the chronic strain of his existence.

Barbara took Albert's hand and tried to pull him to one side, but Albert froze before the giant. The giant stepped closer to Albert and glared down at him. An extreme truth danced lightly in his wide, pale eyes. Other people passed by swiftly, hoping to escape unnoticed. But the giant man in Jockey shorts seemed interested only in Albert and Barbara.

"I am the god Cupid," the man said. He placed his hands on top of Albert's and Barbara's heads. "Kneel before me, my children." His voice was now rich and sonorous, a melodious basso, vibrant with self-confidence.

"Do it," Barbara whispered. "He's nuts."

Albert saw the security guards running toward them. The guards were heavy, slow men. Albert sank to his knees.

"Thus do I bind thee together in the eternal bower," the giant said. The powerful hands of the giant brought Albert's and Barbara's heads together gently. Barbara's face felt cold against his. Albert noticed that the giant's feet were bleeding, as though he'd been walking through broken glass. Barbara squeezed Albert's hand tightly as the giant rotated their heads slowly until they were face to face, lips against lips. "Blessed are they who loveth," he pronounced. Then the security guards arrived and dragged the man away.

"Well, we have one more ride left," Barbara said, dusting off her skirt.

"I don't know," Albert said, his voice shaky. "I don't think I'm up to it."

"Sure you are. He was just a harmless old nut. They thrive around here. The setting appeals to them."

There was a long line in front of Pirates of the Caribbean, but Barbara insisted they get in it. "It moves fast, you'll see," she said.

When it was their turn, they boarded a small, two-person boat that was launched down a dark tunnel. Soon they were out on a subterranean river. Crazed buccaneers leaped out at them from dark crevices, cutlasses brandished high. These were crude robots, their movements too stiff to be believable. Even so, Barbara cringed away from them. Across the water a galleon burst into flames as cannons boomed. Their boat rocked in the churning water. Tongues of real fire licked out at them. Explosions rumbled through the caverns. Bloodthirsty laughter avalanched down from a black, starless sky. Islands of booty glittered in the amber light of torches. The screams of a Spanish princess locked in the brutal arms of a hairy corsair rose above the din. "*¡Ayúdame!*" she called. "*¡Por favor! ¡Ayúdame!*"

Sudden high seas made their boat lurch. A hurricane warning sounded. Barbara fell across Albert's lap. Albert caught her by the shoulders and tried to lift her off, but she didn't move. He watched helplessly as her thin shoulders quaked.

"Barbara?" he said. "Are you crying?"

She lifted her head slightly. Albert saw that her face was wet, that her tears were real and abundant. "I'm *trying* to have fun," she sobbed, miserably. "Honest to Christ, Mr. Court, I am *trying*."

"It's *okay*, Barbara," he said, as the people in the boat ahead of them turned to see what the trouble was.

"It's *not* okay!" Barbara shouted. "God damn you people, can't you understand that it's *not* okay?"

A breeze from the approaching exit cooled Albert's face. "No one holds you responsible, Barbara," he said, surprising himself.

Barbara raised herself and looked at him. "What are you talking about, Mr. Court?"

"Tommy. You couldn't have known, could you? I mean, known what he was going to do. I don't condone what you—"

"Jesus H. Christ on a skateboard," she said.

Albert wiped her face with his handkerchief. He was thinking that her life was probably not as easy as it looked, not nearly as privileged. Those parents of hers, cold as ice and on the climb, socially. "Don't—you shouldn't, Barbara—punish yourself." A tear he had missed sparkled on her chin. He dabbed it away with his handkerchief.

She laughed suddenly and he was shocked by its metallic brilliance. It was an eerily beguiling laugh. It made his scalp tingle. "You silly person," she scolded. "It's *you* I'm crying for, Albert. And me. It's you and me, that's who I'm crying for," she said.

It was dark when they left. In the parking lot, Barbara kissed Albert. He'd been unlocking the car when she slid between him and the door. He tried to back away from her, but her hands locked at the back of his head. He put his hands on her shoulders to force her away, but she yielded so dramatically that he couldn't bring himself to be rough with her. Then her tongue, hard and minty, slid past his lips. He made a sound in his throat, but it didn't deter her. His thick, bewildered tongue met the cool, flexing sweetness of hers hesitantly. She was able to do things with her tongue that had the intricacy of ritual. Then, by strong suction, she pulled his tongue into her mouth. He moved it dumbly, without skill. It was like laboring for speech, and he began to sweat. In the car, he said,

"I'm sorry. I should *not* have done that." His voice was small but passionate with shame.

"Don't be a goof," she said. "We're friends, aren't we?"

Albert bought Tommy a new set of steel-belted radials for his car as a welcome-home present. They stood in the garage looking at the new tires. Tommy was feeling much better. He was a good-looking boy, a fine athlete, and he was intensely humiliated by what he had done to himself. *That slime hole,* he thought. He couldn't believe he'd let a punchboard like Barbara Sunderlin *get* to him. *That crab farm,* he thought. *That pus pit. That walking slit trench.* He ran his hand over the bold tread of the tires. *Fucking Pirellis,* he thought, jubilant. He pictured himself banking into a hairpin curve up in the Sierras, power on, engine winding out, downshifting dramatically to third, the road treacherous with rain, a semi jackknifed across the road ahead, then barreling into the ditch and powering through it, and up the embankment around the trailer, back onto the pavement, *control* a beautiful dream come true, and there, ahead—*check it out*—a lovely woman behind the wheel of a stalled BMW, her hopeful eyes meeting his . . .

Albert, though he loved his son's obvious enthusiasm for the tires, wasn't feeling very well. Guilt and lust had grown in him like twin tumors. He had tried to bury himself with work. He stayed late at the office, studying new software proposals, new marketing areas. He attended engineering meetings that were over his head, sales meetings that didn't concern his territory. But nothing helped. A physical memory of Barbara's busy tongue in the Disneyland parking lot broke his concentration. And to make things worse, to complicate things further, they made plans to see each other again. *What in the hell am I trying to do?* he thought. *Wreck what's left?*

He met her in public places. Beaches, amusement parks, cafés, McDonald's, movie theaters, and Disneyland. They went to Disneyland often and once made love in the back of the submarine when they were the only passengers. He half expected to see the psychotic giant who called himself Cupid, and kept a wary eye whenever they went to the huge amusement park. He could still feel, when he thought about it, the giant's powerful fingers on his skull, forcing his face into Barbara's.

Barbara wrote poems dedicated to him. She mailed them boldly to his house, the envelopes addressed to Alberto Cortazuma. He hid the poems in his workshop and read them at night with the table saw running. The things they did together were gathered in farfetched metaphor and simile.

They exchanged small presents. He bought her a gold bracelet. She bought him garish, hand-painted neckties. She even had herself tattooed for him: flaming lips uttering, by means of a comic-strip balloon, his name.

Pretending to be serious, they discussed eloping to Mexico. In bed, late at night, listening to Sylvia's tranquilized breathing, he would convince himself that they *were* serious, and he would try to visualize the uncomplicated air of the lower Baja.

But he had obligations, duties. *My son, for instance,* he reminded himself. What would Tommy think? How could he expect Tommy not to react with scorn and rage? And then, how could he possibly sleep easy in Mexico knowing the total wreckage he'd left behind? He looked at his son. Tommy was hefting a Pirelli. His tanned biceps were round and hard as apples. Albert loved him. He would give his life for the boy without thinking, without even a sense of martyrdom. A gesture as automatic as a leaf falling in October.

"Tomaso," he said, hoping that speech would not fail him this time.

"Yes, Dad?" Tommy said, glancing at his father quickly, then, just as quickly, looking away. *It's Father-and-Son Time,* he thought, peevish.

Albert wanted to make sure that Barbara was out of the boy's mind, but he wasn't sure how to open the touchy subject. "Deep wounds," he said at last, "sometimes don't heal completely."

Tommy turned his face away from his father so that his smile would not be seen. He picked up another tire, pretended to inspect the tread. "Don't sweat it, Pops," he said. "Old Shit-for-Brains has learned his lesson the hard way."

Albert began to labor. He arched his back and breathed deeply. Tommy looked at him then. "What I mean, Tomaso," Albert said. "What I'm trying to *get* at is, will she—"

"*She?*"

"Don't be annoyed, son. I mean Barbara. Barbara Sunderlin. Will Barbara—"

"Bum me out again? *That* blowjob?"

Albert chewed the inside of his cheek as a stopper moved into his mind. *Rom, rom, rom,* like an audible, high-blood-pressure pulse, richly liquid, staggered him. Then he realized that it *was* his pulse, and that he felt wobbly with vertigo, and the palms of his hands were damp. "Let's get those tires on, Tommy," he said.

Albert dreamed he had fallen out of a hot-air balloon. A rope wrapped itself around his thigh, saving him. But as the supple rope tightened, it made a noose around his genitals. He was hanging from a balloon, high above Disneyland, by his genitals. The pain was spectacular. A crowd of solemn Russians looked up, attracted by his screams.

He woke to find Sylvia pulling his genitals. She had a white-knuckled grip on them. She seemed to be asleep, but her eyes were partly open. She wasn't making a sound other than the slow, deep breathing of a sleeper. He took her by the wrist and tried to remove her hand from him, but she would not release her hold. The pain was severe. He slapped her face as hard as he could from his awkward position, and kept slapping her until she raised her hands to protect herself. Albert got up and went into the bathroom.

After his pain subsided a bit, he found her pills. "Is it one from the blue bottle and two from the red, or vice versa?" he called, but Sylvia didn't answer. He carried the bottles of pills and a glass of water into the bedroom. Sylvia was sitting on the bed with her knees drawn up to her chin. Her eyes were fiercely distrustful.

He put the glass of water and the pills on the night table on her side of the bed. Sylvia's eyes, watchful and bright, like the eyes of a cornered animal, studied his every move, unblinking. Albert put on his bathrobe and Sylvia's eyes darted to each small movement of his hands as he looped and cinched the belt. He glanced at their twenty-three-year-old wedding picture on the dresser. It startled him. Then he went down to his workshop to listen to the saws.

Barbara wanted to go to Palm Springs for the weekend. Albert told LeeAnn, the nurse, that he had to go north on a business trip. Sylvia accepted the story without comment. Dr. Bud Rossetti had changed prescriptions once again, but Sylvia had not improved noticeably. Tommy's return from the hospital did not have the salutary effect Dr. Rossetti was hoping for, either.

"I don't understand it," Albert had told Dr. Rossetti.

"No one does," the doctor admitted, shaking his dark, mournful head slowly. "Christ, Albert, we don't even understand *aspirin*. How can we be expected to grasp acetophenazine maleate?"

"Her breasts have gotten larger."

"A possible side effect."

Albert smiled; the doctor misunderstood it and winked.

"No," Albert said. "I was just thinking. In a sales meeting the other day . . . I sort of went blank. Then someone was tugging at my sleeve. They said that I repeated the words 'motherboard of the mainframe' a couple of dozen times, like a broken record."

"That isn't funny, Albert. It sounds like a symptom, if you want an off-the-cuff opinion."

"Symptom of what?"

"I don't know. Could be a form of Gilles de la Tourette's syndrome. Who can say? It keeps up, you might be a candidate for haloperidol."

"Well, sure, of course," Albert said, his mind elsewhere.

"A sea of troubles," Dr. Rossetti said, sighing massively. He slung his heavy arm around Albert's shoulder. "Look, Albert. Why don't you get Sylvia a nice little dog?"

"Dog?"

"Well, hell! Why not? Do you both good. You never know. A little thing like that might be the missing factor. A lapdog, cuddlesome. A cockapoo, say. One of those little crappy yappers who give you all their love."

Albert stood bewildered before the big, jovial doctor.

Reading Albert's confusion as skepticism, Dr. Rossetti said, "Jesus,

Albert, chemistry isn't everything. We're flesh and blood, after all. We're only human. The next logical step is commitment. That's why I brought up the dog. A goddamned dog might just be the ticket. I've heard of stranger things."

"No dog," Albert said. "Sylvia hates dogs."

The desk clerk was smiling and he wasn't smiling. The smile was in the darkness behind his neutral eyes, not in his face. It was an unassailable smile. Albert, even so, was enraged by it, wherever it was. It was in the clerk's shoulders, his hands, his fastidious movements behind the hotel desk. Albert felt stung by the clerk's abstract smile. *He thinks I'm a forty-nine-year-old man shacking up with a girl young enough to be my daughter,* Albert thought.

In their room, Barbara took her clothes off immediately and went out on the private balcony that overlooked the desert. Albert sat on the bed, watching her move. She was doing a little dance step, a half-unconscious movement generated by a distant radio playing rock. Albert was still mad at the desk clerk. Impudence. As he approached fifty he saw it everywhere. Barbara stopped her little hip-hiking movement and held her arms up to the black desert sky in a gesture that looked like both indecent exposure and worship.

"*Is* it a starry dynamo," she said, "or just a pretty nonsense?"

"What?" Albert said.

She came back into the room, dancing again. The nipples of her breasts were stiff with chill. She stood in front of him, legs apart, hands on the bony shelves of her hips. "Ginsberg," she said. She quoted, " '. . . hundreds of suitcases full of tragedy rocking back and forth waiting to be opened.' "

Albert gave her a wincing smile. "I'm sorry . . . *who?*"

"The old beatnik. *Your* generation, Albert. You ought to remember."

She straddled his lap and forced him backward down on the bed. "Interface ports," he said.

"You got it, handsome," she said.

Later, Albert went into the bathroom and poured Scotch into two plastic cups. Barbara ran down the hall for ice, wrapped in a bed sheet. They sat together on the balcony and sipped their drinks. The stars in the jet-black sky were bright and steady. They made Albert think of a matrix of solder joints on the underside of a circuit board. He laughed a little, then said, "I've been thinking about eloping."

"Eloping?"

"You know. Mexico. We talked about it."

"Quaint," she said, smiling into her drink.

"You're making fun of me," he said.

"No. It *is* quaint. Quaint things turn me on. Like going to a priest and saying *padre*. Or honeymoons. Words like *spellbound* and *womanize*. Gravy is quaint. Pizza. Sock hops and slumber parties. Athletic sweaters. Extramarital affairs. Communists. Vasectomies. The Sears catalog, the Royal Couple, a liberal education. I could go on and on."

"You are really something," Albert said.

Sometime before dawn Barbara whispered into Albert's ear, "How do you think Tommy is going to take this? You and me, I mean."

"Don't make these cruel jokes, Barbara," Albert said.

"Who says I'm joking? I think he should know all about us. I hate deception. It's tacky."

"I said. I said don't."

"Have it your way, Daddy," she said. "But you should know something. Papa's got a bigger crank than his bouncing baby boy, although the kid's got more staying power. It evens out, I guess."

He realized, then, that she *was* just teasing him. "You little *brat*," he said, slapping her thigh gently.

Albert couldn't sleep. He went into the bathroom and made himself another drink. He turned on the ceiling vent. He sat on the edge of the tub and listened to the fan's weak hum. Then he went back into the bedroom.

Barbara was asleep. A shaft of light from the bathroom fell across her neck. Albert knelt beside the bed to kiss her and saw the quick pulse define the artery that ran along her narrow throat. It moved him, and he said her name. Her eyes opened wide. Her face looked very young and frightened. "I'll go anywhere with you, Albert," she said, her voice high and childlike. "I'll do anything you want me to do."

"Maybe," he said. "Maybe you will."

A mass of hot, dry air had moved in from the desert. Tommy couldn't sleep. He got out of bed and loaded *Gaslight* into the disk drive of his Apple. He began the interactive fiction after the fifth unsolved murder. Things were going badly for Scotland Yard. The press was relentlessly critical, and the Queen had called for an internal investigation. Jack the Ripper, whoever he was, had mocked the Yard by sending contemptuous letters to the *Times*. The letters were articulate, witty, and seemed to hold clues that tipped off his future plans. The story switched then, at Tommy's bidding, to a rundown hotel room in Soho. A man and a woman were sitting on a rickety bed. "I knew the instant I saw you that you were not the commonplace slattern," the man said, kissing the woman's hand. While the man's head was bent for the kiss, the woman looked at the ceiling and smiled. Tommy typed in the command for "pause" and asked the program to insert Jack the Ripper's third identity, and to substitute him for the man on the bed. Jack the Ripper's third identity was Dr. Florian Foxglove, respected surgeon. The man on the bed, tubby now and bald, reached into his coat pocket and removed a scalpel.

Sylvia came in carrying a glass of milk. "Oh, good," she said. "I *thought* you were awake. This heat is terrible." She was in her nightgown. "I couldn't sleep, either."

Tommy watched the Ripper cut a neat red smile in the woman's throat, then switched off the machine. "Could I have some of that, Sylvia?" he asked.

Sylvia gave him the glass of milk and Tommy drained it. He wiped his mouth on his pajama sleeve and handed the glass back to his mother.

Sylvia touched his shoulder and squeezed. "I'm so glad you're out of that hospital," she said.

"So am I, Mom," Tommy said. "Did I tell you about the fat guy in the bed next to mine?"

"Do you want some more milk, honey?" she said.

"Sure. But this humongous guy next to me, he *died*. He was a big fat slobbo, always working a crossword puzzle. He died while he was working on one, in fact."

"Oh, no, Tommy, how *awful* for you," she said, leaning down to kiss his hair.

"More like *weird* than awful. He was stuck on a word meaning 'sudden reversal of polarity.' I knew the answer but figured that I'd already spoiled enough of his dumb puzzles by giving him answers. He died straining for the word. I heard his heart *explode,* Sylvia. It sounded like a wet fart, muffled under his blanket and all. It must have lasted about thirty seconds, *fwuuup*. I mean, it was *totally* weird."

Sylvia shuddered. "I wish you hadn't seen such things, honey," she said. Though she was pale, and there were dark hollows under her eyes, she was feeling much better. Dr. Rossetti's latest pre-scription had worked wonders. Her sense of well-being was nearly constant now and could be depended on. The side effects were hardly noticeable. She didn't care at all about the side effects. She was back on her feet and feeling good about things in general, and that was all that mattered. It didn't even bother her that Albert had apparently left home for good. In fact, his unannounced de-parture made her feel lighthearted and giddy. This reaction puzzled her, but Dr. Rossetti's wonderful chemicals wouldn't let her puz-zlement become unmanageable. The future looked bright.

She kissed Tommy's hair again, loving its clean smell and springy strength. She had a wonderful son, a fine, intelligent, handsome son. "I'll get us some more milk," she whispered.

Tommy switched on his computer again. The surgeon, having completed his lethal stroke, held the scalpel gracefully out to one side, at arm's length, the way a conductor of an orchestra would hold his baton to draw out and savor the last sweet outswelling of a symphony.

Culture Shocks

My husband, Whopper, used to call me Swift Premium because of my fat saddlebag thighs, but Thomas Givings once said, "Fat is first among the luxuries, as it hides the humble bones." Thomas called me Cookie, which after all is my given Christian name, thighs or no thighs.

To be honest, I do love to eat. And Whopper, who was no hunger-striker himself, would always heckle me about it. I love nothing better than to take a tray loaded with Tostitos and bean dip and plunk down in front of the TV set and play old Clark Gable movies on the VCR. I will curl up on the sofa and watch *Gone with the Wind, It Happened One Night, Red Dust,* or my all-time favorite, *The Misfits.* All night long sometimes, and into the morning. I would do this when I was still with Whopper, which meant he was alone a lot in our king-size water bed.

Not that he cared. He stopped caring about our marriage the year I passed him in body weight. The morning I saw one-ninety-nine light up between my toes on the digital scale, he said, "Good golly, Miss Molly, your thighs look like Swift Premiums." He laughed at his dumb joke, and the nickname stuck. I was hurt by it, but I didn't go on a crash diet, which can be dangerous. Ask your doctor. I did the opposite. His mean remarks only made me hungrier. I comforted myself with more food.

When we were first married, I was a mere slip of a girl. But married life is fattening. Ask anyone who has tried it. Thomas Givings, who is from some faraway island north or south of New

Guinea or wherever, once said, "Ah, Cookie, the American housewife is married to Big B Boredom Himself. So why should she *not* eat? Savory food in the mouth is never boring."

Truer words were never spoken, even by a white man.

Thomas could be so understanding for a foreigner, especially when compared with Whopper. But Thomas had the advantage of higher education. He wrote a Master's thesis on housewife boredom, called "The Growing Effects of Boredom on the American Housewife." His professors didn't like it much, but not because it wasn't brilliant. Thomas is *very* brilliant, and all the more so when you realize his grandfather lived by throwing wood spears at wild pigs. Whopper, by contrast, never made it out of high school. He was no "brain." He never cracked a book. He was a bodybuilder and more interested in his pecs, lats, quads, and deltoids than he was in English and Math. He would lift three or four hours a day, always watching himself in a full-length mirror. When he passed thirty he began to jog on a treadmill because of his heart. There was nothing wrong with his heart but he'd read somewhere that weight lifting alone didn't do anything for it. He got concerned about things such as blood pressure and fatty deposits in his veins and arteries. He would walk on his treadmill with electrical wires taped to his arms and chest so that he could see his pressure and pulse and whatever else light up in green numbers on a little black box. He would examine himself with his own stethoscope and blood-pressure gadget, his face all puckered like a chimp trying to read the want ads.

Whopper liked the health and exercise shows on TV. Especially the shows about lady bodybuilders. He would whistle me into the rec room so I could watch them pose. This was one of his favorite ways of heckling me about my fat. "Holy smokes," he would say. "Wouldn't one of them cracks give an old boy's choad a proper yank?" (I thought to myself that one of those titless freaks would probably take his choad off at the root just to watch him scream, but I didn't say anything.)

Well, if he believed he was shaming me he was dead wrong. Veiny biceps on a woman's arm is sickening. How ugly can you get? Those female bodybuilders look more like runty men than females of the species. Greased and tanned, those lumpy muscles are just pathetic as they try to imitate man-muscle.

Thomas Givings agreed with me on this point. "A woman," he said, "should not be a replica of a man. A woman should be a delight and a comfort. She should not take on the appearance of a foundry worker. I see this tendency as yet another consequence of profound Big B Boredom Himself."

Thomas has that lowdown mellow type of Darth Vader voice, like the one you hear on the 7-Up commercials. When I first heard him speak I got the chills. He would also sprinkle his conversation with foreign words and phrases, such as, "Life, *ma chérie*"—that's French—"without the higher material satisfactions, be they a canoe full of sacred yams, a freezer laden with top sirloin, or a fine automobile in the garage, is mere subsistence. This invariably leads to profound Big B Boredom Himself. Surely the gods did not intend for us to live only for the sake of the marginal life, don't you agree?"

He tended to run ahead of me. "Hell yes," I said, hoping that blurting out my agreement would cover up my ignorance.

But he liked to keep me over the fire. "What, then, Cookie, is the result of such a life?"

"Well, like you just said, Thomas. Profound Big B Boredom."

"Himself."

"Right. Himself."

"He *exists,* you know. He is a god, perhaps the most potent god in America. This is the central theme of my thesis."

I looked at him and he looked at me. I couldn't tell if he was pulling my leg or what. But his long, unblinking stare led me to believe he was serious. So I said, "Is that a fact." Thomas had this way of teaching things to me that never exactly seemed like teaching. I don't think I learned much, though.

"It is more than a fact," he said. "The average rainfall in Orange County is a *fact.* I am speaking of things that are not just observably true. I am speaking of the infinitely mysterious."

I ran that around in my head for a while but came up empty. "Oh," I said. "How fascinating."

Things that got to me didn't get to him, and vice versa. Traffic, for instance. I hate it. Especially when it piles up on a hot, smoggy day. Once we sat in a five o'clock jam on the Santa Ana Freeway in ninety-seven-degree heat and Stage One Smog, and he just talked and talked about Life and such as if we were out on a cool patio sipping lemonade. He got out of the car and walked around for a while among the sorehead commuters, smiling that happy smile he has when things are going right for him, and taking scientific notes. He wants to be an anthropologist, and will be someday, in spite of his setbacks, which I'll get into later.

He is also studying business administration and hopes someday to start up a chain of fast-food franchises called SAM'S YAMS. He is very big on yams and thinks America should be, too. There is no Sam, or there wasn't one then, but you'll hear more about that later, too.

He is a self-satisfied man. He told me this. He said that it was a crying shame that self-satisfaction has come to mean *smug*. "If a man is not satisfied with himself, *ma petite chou*"—French again—"then why should anyone else find cause to be pleased with the wretched fellow?"

Whopper was never satisfied with himself or with anyone else. Especially me. His nickname makes you think of a big, porky guy full of fun with a happy-go-lucky attitude. But he was just the opposite. You could not trim an ounce of casual fat off him. He was dead-serious muscle from earlobes to corns. "Whopper" is just a high school name that stuck. He got it for his reputation as a hamburger-eating champ. He and his friends would go down to the local Burger King and he would eat five or six Whoppers in a row, gobbling them in two or three bites each, chugging quarts of Dr Pepper to wash them down. They called him Jaws, Deep Throat, Godzilla, and Death Star, but then settled for Whopper, which only made sense. He could eat and eat and not get fat because of his constant weight lifting. Whereas someone like me can just read a label on a jar of guacamole dip and gain a pound. You have probably seen my type of girl before, blocking the aisle in Safeway or standing in line at Mr. Steak, stomach growling.

Thomas Givings is no small eater himself. But he is one of those metabolism types who will never gain. He is tall and thin and his teeth are so square and strong they give you chills when he smiles. Though he is over thirty years old, the college he goes to gave him a track scholarship because he is so naturally good at throwing the javelin. "It comes from thousands of years, *Liebchen*"—German, I think—"of hunting small animals with spears. There is a decided Lysenkoistic aspect to evolution, don't you agree?"

He must have seen my eyes go dull but he didn't say anything, just waited. So I shrugged. "You bet," I said.

Then he smiled. "Ah, Cookie, you did not study your lessons in school very thoroughly. Lysenko was the Soviet biologist, discredited in the West, who held that acquired characteristics are inheritable, from parents to offspring. He was compelled by the unfortunate policies of the Communist regime to ignore the importance of the chromosomes and genes. And though I despise Stalinist methods, who can say that Lysenko was totally wrong? Perhaps the genetic materials are able to learn from the external environment itself, *n'est-ce pas?*"

I got the idea that he was playing with me. "Nest paw yourself, Thomas," I said, slapping the air between us as though his words had become gnats.

Thomas is a dark man, not exactly Negro-dark, but dark like that, but also *white*-looking in a way, with hard black hair that storms out of his head, rippling back, as if he's standing in a hurricane, and a long, thin nose with some type of "designer" scars dotting his high cheeks. He is very handsome. Especially since he wears a trim Clark Gable type of mustache, which I always like to see on a man's lip.

He lives in a bare little house near his college which he calls his "base camp" because it is from this little place that he goes out to study our native culture for his thesis. He has a narrow backyard where he grows his crazy yams. He calls them "sacred," since they mean something besides food to the people of his home island. Yams of all sizes and shapes, yams like I have never seen before, yams that I doubt are yams at all. He grows yams that are as small as your thumb and yams that look like torpedoes. He treats them like people, even going so far as to talk to them, or *sing*. He will kneel in the earth and sing little songs, and once I saw a tear roll down his scars as he lullabied the ground.

Goofy. But then I imagine that a lot of the things *we* do must seem goofy to foreign eyes.

But you cannot fault him for his manners. He is the perfect gentleman in all ways. He has good taste in music and art and magazines. He knows all about American movies. He knows more about them than I do and I grew up on them. "I don't like," he said, "the antibusiness tenor of the sentimental socialist directors of the 1930s. Take, for instance, the subtheme of *It's a Wonderful Life*. It simply states that the successful businessman, in order to *be* successful, must also be without moral scruples. This is patent nonsense, just as its corollary is nonsense, namely that the businessman who is *not* successful is necessarily lovable. Claptrap, Cookie. A foolish myth at best, populist propaganda at worst. You see?"

He told me this at Denny's. We ate at Denny's a lot. He said he was studying their methods because he wanted SAM'S YAMS to be just as successful as Denny's. He liked Denny's generous portions. He said the keys to a successful fast-food franchise are generous portions, speed, and quality. Pretty much in that order.

I like to watch him eat, he is so neat and well mannered. When he sits down at a table, he arranges his napkin so carefully in his lap that you realize the truth of his words: "The *way* you eat is just as important as *what* you eat. Taking food," he said, "in the communal arrangement"—anthropology talk—"is a fundamentally spiritual exercise that propagates itself into seemingly unrelated areas of one's existence. Food, Cookie, consists of various and sundry compounds of the carbon atom. If one understands this, one shall come to realize that the difference between *canard à l'orange*"—a French dish—"and foot-long chilidogs is but a matter of molecular arrangement. The diner, Cookie, transcends the dinner. Eating the raw brains of an unweaned child in one area of the world will impart spiritual powers when accomplished according to a well-defined ritual. Whereas, a pork-chop sandwich eaten with unconscious lust in Los Angeles has the potential to distribute hungry metaphysical moths along the soul's silky seams."

That almost made me barf, the part about eating raw baby brains, because I was in the middle of a bowl of chili con carne. I guess he saw me turn white because he changed the subject to his studies in grad school. He told me he was studying our culture in the way that Margaret Mead and Ruth Benedict and others had studied his, or cultures like his. I had never heard of them and I told him so. He couldn't believe his ears. He rolled his eyes and fanned his face with his napkin. He made a little scene right there in Denny's. He pretended to choke and he accidentally spit some slaw across the table. "Tell me, *please,*" he said, "tell me, Cookie, that you are joking."

I got red in the face, I think, because I felt my temper coming up. I do have a temper, though it has a very high boiling point, about seven hundred degrees. "So I'm uneducated," I said. "So what?"

He backed off then and went on to explain who those women were and what they did that was so important. He called them paragons of the profession. And then he called himself one of their chickens who had come home to roost. "I am looking up through the microscope at the big blue eye of Western Civilization," he said.

We had a lot of crazy dates, like spending the afternoon in K mart or White Front. Whopper didn't care one way or the other, although he had never seen Thomas. He didn't ask any questions and I didn't offer any answers. Besides, he had his own social life, which I will get into later.

Once, when we were in K mart, and the girl had just loaded the glass deli bin with fresh hot chickens, I said, "Oh, Thomas, even the *smell* of food is fattening to me!"

He patted my arm and smiled gently with a faraway look in his red-brown eyes. "Take heart, Cookie," he said. "Incorporated into your ample form are the bold energies and aggrandizing logics of your highly aggressive culture. I find you immeasurably attractive for this selfsame reason."

You know how people from big cities such as New York will talk loud and not care who hears them? Well, Thomas is like that, even though he is not from any city. So, heads turned when he said these things to me. It embarrassed me a little, but he didn't notice a thing.

"It's unfair, though," I said, half whispering.

He threw his head back and laughed out loud. That big Darth Vader laugh, and the crowd around us stopped cold to watch. It didn't bother him a bit—about the crowd, I mean. In fact he seemed to like an audience. "There *is* no 'fair' and there is no 'unfair,' " he said.

I pulled him away from the crowd. "Just what does *that* mean, Professor?" I said, miffed in spite of my embarrassment.

"Simply that, in my native tongue, there is no word for 'fair,' and, in consequence, there is no word for 'unfair.' *Capish?*"

(Italian.) I laughed. The crowd, who were sticking with us, also laughed. A big guy in a Levi jacket and cowboy boots said, "What a *load.*"

"Thomas," I said. "How could anyone *not* have a word for 'fair' or 'unfair'? It doesn't make sense. It's like not having a word for 'hot' or for 'cold.' "

"To the contrary," he said, switching on a big projection-type TV set. (We had wandered from the deli section to the big appliances, with about a dozen people in tow. I guess they were curious about this tall, skinny, black South Sea Islander in a three-piece suit with wild hair and crazy scars peppering his face, and his two-ton white girlfriend.) "It makes fine sense, Cookie." He chuckled deep in his thin chest, and then, like some kind of miracle or practical joke, the 7-Up guy comes on the big-screen TV set, laughing along with Thomas.

"*I* don't think it makes sense," said the big guy in the Levi jacket. He looked kind of mean to me and his tone was definitely threatening. He may have been one of those racial-purity types who do not believe in mixing.

"Let me ask you this question, then," Thomas said to us. "Do you have a word in your admirable language that describes the sensation in one's liver when a hostile shaman chants a spell that will transform one into a bush pig?"

The man in the Levi jacket said *shit* but left off the *t* so that he wouldn't offend anyone. I said, "That's the dumbest thing I have ever heard."

But Thomas went on with it. "You have no word for it," he said, his voice booming so that it must have carried past the big appliances over to the power saws and drills, "because the experience does not exist in your culture."

"Not so *loud,* Thomas," I whispered, yanking at his coat.

But he was on a roll. "Fairness, Cookie, like all abstract concepts, does not exist. It is an English self-delusion. It justified an Empire. Let me explain: English justice, English religion, English manners— all these things would be given to the poor backward races in place of their wretched superstitions and barbaric customs. A *fair* exchange, you see? Exchange for what? For gold, Cookie. For diamonds, for crude oil, for rubber trees and tin mines, for silk and teak, for cheap labor, and so on. Then they proceeded to convince themselves that they had bestowed the more valuable gift."

"They *did,* asshole," said the man in the Levi jacket, losing his patience.

"But fair is still fair, Thomas," I said.

"Only in cricket. The Spanish *conquistadores* were more honest with themselves. 'We want your national wealth, you little feathered men,' they said. 'In exchange, we offer you our fine Hispanic bottoms to kiss.' That was their attitude. It was of course the British attitude as well, but they could not admit it to themselves because of this necessary concept of *fairness* they pay lip service to. Oh, the rule of paradox is not limited to the English. It occurs everywhere on earth, even among the primitives. It is just one of those cultural conundrums; a curiosity. Do not misunderstand me, I am not castigating the English race."

"This is one fancy-talking darky," the man in the Levi jacket said, his face ugly mean and red.

For the first time, Thomas seemed to be aware of the fact that in America it isn't a good idea to give highbrow-type lectures in K mart on a Saturday afternoon. He suddenly looked a little gray. But then he turned back to the big TV set and began switching channels until he landed on a football game, the Bears against the

Eagles, and a touchdown had just been scored and the crowd was screaming because a ref had dropped a penalty flag. Everyone's attention, including the big mean guy's, went to the game, and Thomas and I got out of there.

Out in the parking lot, I said, "You're impossible, Thomas."

I didn't mean to offend him, but he looked glum. "Your impossibilities are not my impossibilities," he said sadly.

"Vice versa," I said, in Latin.

Did I tell you just how tall Thomas is? He might be as tall as six feet six. Or did I mention how odd we looked together, since I am only five feet two? As we left K mart I saw ourselves in the plate-glass window and would have laughed out loud if it had been someone else. Before he started calling me Swift Premium, Whopper sometimes called me Brunswick, after the bowling ball.

I looked up at his long, sad face as we walked slowly to his beat-up Nash Rambler. "I'm sorry, Thomas," I said, not sure what I was apologizing for. "I guess I'm just dumb and fat and not worth your time."

We got in the old car and he plugged a tape into the deck he had wired into the dashboard. It was his favorite American music, Mantovani. He likes the strings and the slow rhythms. It relaxes him, he says, because it reminds him of the wind as it blows through the tall coconut palms of his home island.

He sighed. "The carbon atom, having at last achieved consciousness, attempts to articulate its remorse," he said. "A ludicrous display."

"Are you trying to insult me?" I said. He sometimes gets snotty when he's blue. But it's always egghead-snotty, so you're never exactly sure how he means it.

"No, no, Cookie," he said. "I include myself in my rather flippant analysis."

Which was only proper, as he can be pretty dumb sometimes himself. Like the time he came to visit me at home (Whopper was still at work) and I got out the camcorder and took his picture as he left his Nash and came up the walkway to the house. The walkway is made out of flagstones set into the lawn, and he stepped gingerly from one to another as if they were rocks studding a river and he had to worry about slipping into the rapids. He was carrying his briefcase in one hand and a box of candy in the other. When I said, "Come in, Thomas," he walked right into a close-up before he saw my camcorder. And when I played the tape on the big TV set he got depressed and begged me to erase it. I asked him why but he just got more down in the mouth, mumbling something about losing a piece of his soul, until the only way I could save the afternoon was to erase him.

There is this Swift Premium like myself on TV. It's an ad for some diet center. The Swift Premium is sneaking cookies when her ten-year-old brat daughter comes up from behind and says, "*Don't,* Mother!" as if the fatty had taken down the rat poison to end her weight problem once and for all. Then the snot shows her jowly mother a newspaper item about this diet clinic where the lardo can sit down with a trained counselor who will root out the *real* problem that makes her eat all the time, which of course is never just appetite alone, is it?

Thomas Givings said a lot of women on his island are fat and yet the men don't hold it against them. In fact, most men consider fat as a sign of a generous soul. A fat woman is thought to be best in the marriage bed, greedy for pleasure, and they are tireless. They are also comfortable to lie down on. He actually said this to me.

This was back when we first met. He didn't mean to be fresh, but we were not even on a first-name basis. And here he was talking about the marriage bed. It was all high-minded, but even so he let his eyes roam from my keggy thighs, to my hips, up to my stuffed blouse. As he looked, his fine nostrils opened. I'm telling you he was breathing hard. Givings is a name he took from the Pomona phone book. His real name is Malu Manny You Too, or something approximate.

Whopper could never see me the way Thomas does. He was disgusted by my fat. He finally threatened to get himself a girlfriend if I didn't shape up. And when I didn't, he followed through on his promise. He nicknamed her Lean Cuisine out of spite. And, out of spite, he brought her home.

"Lean Cuisine," he said, "I'd like you to meet Swift Premium."

He thought he was funny. But this girl he called Lean Cuisine was so skinny she looked half dead. You could see the pitted surface of her shinbones through her transparent, fatless skin. Her head looked like a child's skull with tissue paper stretched over it. I didn't consider her pretty at all. I don't think Whopper did either. He just wanted to use her. You have seen her type in a bikini on the beach tanned some dying shade of beige and barely strong enough to lift the volleyball. If she weighed ninety pounds I'd be surprised. She just stood there in my living room, a slump-shouldered skeleton with sick, flat eyes fixed in a bored-to-death-since-birth look. And yet *I* was supposed to feel like the freak.

That's when I started going to night school. I had to do something with my life to make it seem there was an original reason for it. I think the richest and most fortunate people in the world are the ones who knew what they wanted to be when they were young, and just went out and made their dream come true. Besides, I was getting tired of watching the same old movies on the VCR while Whopper and Lean Cuisine were running around in his car, the *real* joy of his life, a sleek Turbo Daytona coupe.

So, I took Introduction to the Stock Market just for the heck of it, and that's where I met Thomas. I didn't know the difference between the stock market and the supermarket and couldn't have told anyone the difference between a municipal bond and a bail bond, and thought it would be a good place to begin my general education.

One night a group of us from the class went to Denny's for coffee. People drifted away until it was only me and Thomas in the booth. I had ordered the hot apple fritter with vanilla ice cream on top. He had Mexican-style fried ice cream. How can I forget his very first words to me in that booth? "I must say, madame, if you will forgive the impertinence. But I find your unabashed enthusiasm for food most admirable, not to say unusual for this culture." That's what he said.

I stirred some Sweet 'n Low into my coffee, giving myself a little time to sort out his meaning. But, like the dummy I was back then, I said, "Come again, Doc?"

He laughed—the big laugh that had heads turning our way in

surprise thinking that Darth Vader had stepped into Denny's—and waved his long, slender hand as if to shoo a fly away from his face. "No, no, I am no doctor, madame. Not yet, at any rate. The doctor of philosophy degree shall have to wait until such time as I am financially able to support a long and arduous endeavor at one of your better universities, such as Harvard."

That's why, he said, he was studying the stock market. He told me about his future business plans, how much sheer opportunity this country had to offer. The fast-food-franchise market had barely been scratched, according to Thomas. He told me about his plans to sell yams—yams on a stick, deep-fried yams, whipped yams in a tub topped with a dab of yogurt, candied yams—and he told me about the health benefits of yams and how this country was becoming more and more health-conscious, and the yam, packed with the beta-carotenes and vitamin A as well as a good variety of minerals, was the perfect health food and could be legally advertised as such. He said he would make a fortune within a few years, four or five at most.

He got more and more excited as he talked. He was crazy about the stock market. "The bull mood is going to continue for several more years, perhaps until the end of this century. Now is the time to take advantage of it, madame," he said. "I would not, however, buy very many interest-sensitive issues at this time," he said, as if I had set my mind on doing such a thing. "I do not trust the Fed completely—I have heard rumors of a tightened fiscal policy, which, of course, would mean a resurgence of the prime." He told me how he admired men like T. Boone Pickens, the master of the takeover bid.

I guess I was just staring at him like a dummy. I hadn't heard of T. Boone Pickens—just as I hadn't heard of Margaret Mead or Ruth Benedict. But he took my blank face as doubt and said, "So, you do not approve of the takeover stratagem? Listen, at this very moment, the restaurant we are sitting in, Denny's, is in danger of being swallowed by the Marriott group, which has swallowed other smaller fish recently, such as the Roy Rogers chain and Winchell's Dough Nuts. It is a fish-eat-fish nation, it is very American to conduct business this way. One need not feel sorry for the small fishes. We shall still have our cake and pie and the waitresses shall be tipped."

"It all sounds like pig greed," I said.

"Ah. It is a great mistake to pretend that pig greed does not exist. One might as well deny the existence of sexual passion, another product of selfish need."

He was sweating. So was I. "What about the future?" I said, not sure exactly what I meant. I felt flustered.

"*Never* to worry." He laughed. "The best indicator of just how healthy this country is, madame, is foreign investment. The Japanese, who preside over a tremendous liquidity, have invested ten percent of it in America. We are speaking of billions and billions of dollars."

Tiny beads of sweat glazed his forehead and upper lip, and his eyes were wild-looking. He was breathing too hard. "You are going to hyperventilate," I said, laughing. He laughed a little, too, but in the next second his eyes rolled back and his eyelids fluttered. He gripped the table with both hands, causing our coffee cups to jump and slosh over.

"What's the matter, Mr. . . . ?" I said, realizing that I didn't know either of his names.

"Givings," he said. "Thomas Givings, at your service, madame." He was trying to be cool, but he was coming unglued, anyone could see that.

I didn't know what to do. So I picked up his hand and started rubbing it. It seemed to help. He started taking deep breaths, making little singing sounds as he let the air out.

"Are you going to be all right, Thomas?" I said.

His eyes tried to find my face, as if there were a few dozen people sitting opposite him. He gave me a quarter. "Would you please, madame, go to the jukebox and play a Mantovani record for me? It would help."

I shrugged. "Sure," I said. "Anything in particular?"

"They have only one. 'Fly Me to the Moon.' It is not my favorite, but it will have to do."

I played it, and sure enough, he began to breathe easier.

"I am very much afraid that I have contracted one of your

indigenous diseases, madame," he said, mopping away the glaze of sweat from his brow.

I leaned away from him. "It's not catching, is it?"

He smiled—that big, lovely, square-toothed smile. "It may be, I wouldn't know. Your famed Dr. Freud called it Anxiety Neurosis. It is a general apprehensiveness, a free-floating nervous condition. I should be more cautious."

I *had* heard of Dr. Freud. "Oh *dear,*" I said.

"My goodness, my goodness," he said, rocking from side to side a little.

I gripped his hand hard. His eyes rolled back again. "I *wish* it weren't 'Fly Me to the Moon,' " he said. "I wish it were 'Long Ago and Far Away.' "

He pulled his hand free of mine and began to wave at the invisible fly again. "Do not be overly concerned," he said. "It is nearly gone. What I truly fear is that the disease will progress to specific phobias. That is always a dread possibility. Fear of water. Fear of caterpillars. Fear of crossing bridges. Fear of dark places."

He moaned, and I found myself moaning too, not as loud, but I really felt sorry for him at that moment.

"Oh, madame," he said. "I do not wish to become phobic!"

"Who *does?*" I said, a little helplessly.

He stood up, but he was shaky. I steered him out of Denny's. He pointed to his Nash. Then told me he couldn't possibly drive it. He climbed into the backseat and curled up in a tight little ball. From his curled-up position he handed me the keys. How someone six feet six inches tall could make himself look like a carsick child is beyond me, but he did it. I drove him to the address he gave me. That's how our famous romance got its start.

Whenever I saw him after that, I tried to keep the conversation away from the stock market and the future of the American economy. It got him too excited. Our dates at first were mostly movie dates. After a movie, we would go to his little house by the college for snacks. It was one of those 1930s bungalows, tiny and run-down. It seemed to still have all of its 1930 sadness. He had modern furniture but it didn't help. The furniture came from one of those discount warehouses—imitation this, simulated that. Vinyl that looked like crushed leather. Plastic that looked like richly grained wood. He had a good TV set complete with cable hookup, and a big stereo. His collection of Mantovani records was the biggest I've ever seen. He must have had thirty or more Mantovani albums. The kitchen was decent and had a built-in microwave, four-burner range, and breakfast nook. His bedroom, though, was primitive. Just a straw mat on the floor, stacked cardboard boxes for a dresser, and the walls were bare except for the masks.

There were about a dozen masks, carved out of wood and painted with all the colors of the rainbow, hanging on the wall over the straw mat. He called them his Dancing Masks. They represented the gods of his people, and a dancer, wearing one of the masks, would *become* that god by dancing himself into a trance. Sometimes he'd put one of his Dancing Masks on and we'd listen to Mantovani or watch TV and talk. His favorite mask had two mouths. When he talked while wearing this mask his voice became two voices, one high-pitched and the other low-pitched. The two voices harmonized with each other and made a pretty, fluting sound. He would dance while wearing this mask, too. Kind of a bent-knee, herky-jerky, gooseneck dance that never failed to make me a little nervous. He seemed so different when he danced—native, I mean—as if his fine three-piece suit and cultivated ways were so much tinsel.

"It was the two-voiced god you saw, Cookie," he said, when I told him how strange his dance made me feel. "Thomas Givings, so called, became absent. The god helps me with all the things I must do in your country."

But the god didn't help him enough. The college rejected his Master's thesis. He got depressed and his anxiety attacks came more often. He would play Mantovani records at full volume, since they were the only things that helped him through his hard times. Dancing in the mask of the two-voiced god didn't relax him, as it once had, and so he quit doing it. He lost his faith.

He was gloomy and untalkative. I tried to cheer him up but only made him mad. He threw his thesis at me. It didn't hit me, and he didn't mean for it to, but it landed with a loud slap on the sofa next to me. He glowered at me as if to make me understand that his failed thesis was somehow my fault. So I picked it up and thumbed through it—it was only about fifty pages long—and saw the part about me. Yes, I was one of the American housewives he was studying. I wondered how many other housewives he had "studied." The part about me was dog-eared and underlined in red by the professor who flunked him out of graduate school. I read: "The subject's unfailing enthusiasm for foods of any description, regardless of nutritive value, is incontestable evidence of the presence of the Great God Boredom, with all his shadowy ubiquity, in the life of the average American housewife. He has settled profoundly into the center of her alimentary regions and calls for continual offerings, be they Spam and hotcakes or Twinkies and Ding Dongs." In the margins the professor had written in neat red ink, ". . . nebulous, however poetic, if one will grant the metaphor, but *hardly* a specimen of scientific fieldwork."

"I am the victim," Thomas said, "of intercultural misconceptions, if not naked prejudice."

"I'm sorry," I said, as if it were all my fault, then added, more sharply than I should have, "It's not *fair,* is it, Thomas?"

He winced. "Your sympathy is ignorant of my profound defeat, and therefore of limited value," he said. A spiteful light gleamed meanly in his eyes. *"Acta est fabula.* It is all over, Cookie."

I got up to leave. In the doorway, I decided to drop my little bomb. "I think I'm pregnant, Thomas," I said.

He looked at me for a long moment, then slapped his forehead. He ran to his stereo and put on Mantovani at full volume, then curled up in a tight, childlike ball on the couch, his arms covering his head. He knew he had to be the one.

I left his house and started walking. Do I have to tell you I was crying my head off? Probably not. Thomas Givings had taken all my love, and I had a lot to give. I love him to this day and still meet him now and then at Denny's, though there is a carefully held distance between us. He's doing another thesis, but I haven't asked what it's about. Should I care? Probably not.

It's possible he still loves me, too, if he ever did. But it's also clear to me that every culture in the world has its own version of love, and no two versions make much sense to each other. A bridge has to be built from both sides, and more often than not the two halves don't quite meet. When you try to cross over you fall into the river, where it's sink or swim.

I'm a swimmer. I know that now. Fat makes you buoyant. Of course Whopper is out of my life, and that's no big loss. I live in an apartment across the street from the law offices where I work—as a cleaning lady. If I said I was a fat *and* happy cleaning lady, would you believe me? Probably not. *"C'est la vie,"* as Thomas would say. But listen, I have my TV, my VCR, my collection of Gable films, and a goddamn big refrigerator. And I have my little boy, Sam, named after Thomas's dream of boarding the American gravy train. Sam and I have some good times, and even though he's still a crawler, I can tell he's got his daddy's intelligence. You can see intelligence glowing in his eyes.

Sam loves stories. I've got some pretty good fairy tales to tell him. Like the time his daddy cooked up some of his sacred yams for us. I don't tell him that I believe that his daddy would have been considered buggy even by his own people. But one thing he could do that every culture in the world would recognize as sane, and that's garden. His yams were beautiful.

He cooked up the yams in his microwave. They were big, dark, perfect-looking yams. He served them on a plate, along with a little white wine. The table was lit by candles, and Mantovani's strings gave everything a perfect calm.

I opened a big yam with my knife. A mini-geyser of steam shot up out of it. I cut it wide and laid in a pad of butter.

"Speak to him," Thomas said. "Tell him you like him. Apologize for cutting him and for biting into his body and for chewing his sweet orange flesh."

"I will *not*," I said, laughing. But I did, anyway, because I'm such a willing fool.

I stuffed myself on those yams. So did Thomas. We became very drowsy and contented. Later that evening, if my arithmetic is correct, little Sam was conceived.

"These were magical yams, Cookie," Thomas said, his eyelids heavy.

I burped a little. "Sure," I said.

Thomas put on one of his masks, a smoky-blue affair with thin slits for eyes and a black dot for a mouth. His voice came out of it needle-thin. "My wart, too, my one ear, too," he said. He said it four or five times, chanting it, dancing a brief, stiff-kneed shuffle.

"Come again?" I said, then realized it wasn't English.

"We are now quite invisible, Cookie," he said, taking off the mask.

"*Ipse dixit,*" I said, which means, in Latin, I hear you talking, Buster.

"It's true, Cookie. We are transparent as the wind."

Mantovani, as if by perfect timing, began playing "Where Are You?" The back of my neck got tingly. I said, "But I can see you, and you can see me."

"Yes, but to all others we are invisible."

"We're alone. There are no others."

"That has little to do with it, *ma bien-aimée fille,*" he said. "We are also becoming insubstantial, weightless as the air around us, thin as the skin of a bubble."

When I tell this story to little Sam, I leave out my skepticism. I tell him that it never mattered to me that there was no one else there not to see us, or to feel the warm, humid air of us wash against his face as we drifted out of our chairs, toward the bedroom, and into the unbelievable heart of everything.

Romance:
A Prose Villanelle

*I*f this was not meant to be, then nothing was meant to be. Sometimes when two strangers meet they feel they've known each other forever. The tall man in cowboy regalia was such a person to Marianna. She quivered involuntarily, like the delicate needle of a compass, before the quiet magnetism of his masculine presence. A sleeping passion stirred restlessly in her neglected loins. Was he the man she'd envisioned years ago in the hazy longing of adolescent daydreams—a vision dismissed a few years later as the pubescent fantasy of an imaginative child? More to the point, was he her type? But what *was* one's "type"? Of this she had no idea. Years of carefully managed emotions had dulled her judgment in these matters. For to know one's type is to know one's needs. Marianna Kensington was a desert of unknown needs that any random flood might violate into bloom.

After years of indifferent love from a man she'd lost all respect for, Marianna had ventured west to begin her life anew. As she deplaned at the Albuquerque airport and entered the terminal, a chill of anticipation had made her shiver despite the horizon-warping heat of the southwestern desert. Though she was forty now, she had lost nothing of her superbly svelte yet roundly voluptuous figure, which her husband, Kenneth, had nagged her to conceal, even though he no longer responded to it. And conceal it she did—in bulky knit sweaters with high necks, in voluminous stretch pants designed to hide matronly thighs and backsides, and in unfashionable but "sensible" shoes with good supports. Kenneth wanted, above all, for Marianna to project the image of the efficient house-wife, the dedicated mother, the resourceful community volunteer. It was important to his self-image that she be regarded as a paragon of domestic reliability and propriety. For her part, Marianna was compliant as potter's clay. She allowed Kenneth to mold her with his hectoring demands, making her fit each image he believed enhanced his career as deputy advisor to the assistant mayor.

She'd walked away from a twenty-year marriage without regret. The children were grown and gone. She still had time, she felt, to find out who Marianna Kensington was. Perhaps she was no one. How frightening! But how much more frightening to deceive yourself into thinking you were complete when in fact you were nothing but a blank page waiting to be filled in! The suburbs were crowded with safe and comfortable women who were essentially blank pages waiting for a violating pen. Silence was their chief enemy. For silence could let the inner emptiness rise to the surface, like a submerged but featureless continent. And so they filled each waking hour with gossip and chat, with shopping, and with the tedium of domestic chores. The resented demands of children were, in fact, a necessary barrier reef that prevented the intrusion of that dangerous silence. The famous "empty-nest syndrome" was but a high-toned euphemism that denoted the terrifying enemy, Silence, who, given a small opportunity, would enter the house and sit down like a bold intruder. The intruder smiles with his superior knowledge of the little dark mechanisms of your heart. Ignoring him, you pick up the latest Silhouette or Harlequin Romance and try to read, but the words blur together, passion links arms with despair—jealousy, anger, spite, kink up like a bicycle chain that throws itself loose from its sprocket and the whole enterprise coasts to a dismal stop halfway to nowhere. You skip ahead to the forlorn sobs of the heroine as the handsome but brutal horseman rips her blouse to the waist, or takes her roughly in an autumn copse, or more gently but with degrading insouciance in the elegantly appointed drawing room of his antebellum mansion. It doesn't help. The silence you have contrived successfully all your life to hold at bay slips in between the lines of bloated prose, it invades each preposterous scene or trumped-up emotion, it collects in the gaps between chapters. And it is there, waiting for you at the end, in the gritty dead-white paper, rustling patiently with the last word.

"My name is Jeff Granger," the tall cowboy said. "I'm foreman out at the Y Bar Y. You'll be cooking for my crew." She put down her valise and extended her hand. He took it in his and something like an electrical current passed between them in a hard, shocking vibration. She wondered if he felt it. It embarrassed her, and when he released her hand, a wave of dizziness almost overcame her. His hand had been hard and callused, its great strength had been apparent, and yet it had been gentle and warm. "Jorge Méndez here will be your assistant," he continued, his voice edged now with a wariness and Marianna knew that he, too, had felt the vibrant current pass between them. A short heavyset man of mixed blood who had been standing behind Jeff and off to one side stepped forward holding his wide-brim straw hat in his brown hands. "*Buenos días, señora,*" he said, with an almost courtly deference, but in his Indian-black eyes Marianna thought she saw a flicker of icy resentment.

Marianna had answered an ad that for some reason had been placed in the *Boston Globe*: "Wanted, Ranch Cook. Hard work. Fair pay. Some benefits. Healthiest life-style going." Her marriage to Kenneth was finished as far as she was concerned. Kenneth had raged and threatened, but she had met this display with unruffled calm, and all his fury came to nothing, like a dry summer storm that begins with the promise of deluge but offers only a few strokes of lightning and an afternoon of darkened skies. When his rage turned to abject pleading, her cold resolve became colder and more resolute. She realized then that there had never been anything to love in this man. What she'd once believed was strength she now saw as headstrong infantile petulance. What she'd taken as love was only his bottomless need for constant reassurance and praise. What she once saw as his intelligent commitment to honorable ideals she now saw as commonplace ambition. In mid-life she had been given the ability to see things for what they were. Her two children, Annie and Ken

Junior, were away at college. There was no reason to stay and every reason to go. A ranch in New Mexico seemed as good a place as any to start a brand-new life. She climbed into Jeff Granger's beat-up Ford Bronco with a clear sense of leaving her old life and starting her new one. Jeff knocked his dusty Stetson back on his head, revealing a rich shock of wavy chestnut hair, a few strands of which were pressed to his forehead with honest sweat. He smiled at her as she settled into the seat beside him and Marianna's heart suddenly felt too big for her chest.

If this was not meant to be, then nothing was meant to be. Sometimes when two strangers meet they feel they've known each other forever. Jeff Granger was such a man to Marianna. She quivered before the quiet magnetism of his masculine presence. A sleeping passion stirred restlessly in her neglected loins. Was he the man she'd envisioned years ago? More to the point, was he her type? What *was* one's type? She had no idea. Years of careful emotions had dulled her judgment. For to know one's type is to know one's needs. Marianna was a desert of unknown needs that any random flood might violate into bloom.

The ride out to the Y Bar Y was bone-jolting rough. Jeff drove with one careless hand on the wheel at high speed, heedless of the rutted road. Marianna held on to the door handle and more than once had to steady herself by grabbing his shoulder. "What's the hurry?" she'd wanted to say, but didn't. She was now an employee of a large cattle ranch and not in a position to criticize the foreman. In the back of the Bronco, Jorge Méndez dozed. Jeff played country and western tunes on the tape deck at high volume. It occurred to Marianna that this was a rude thing to do since it preempted any attempt at civil conversation. It was as if Jeff were saying, *I don't want to talk to you, what you have to say doesn't interest me.* She tried to shout a question about the countryside, but either he didn't hear her or he pretended not to. *He doesn't approve of me,* she thought. She concluded it had not been his idea to run the ad in the *Boston Globe* for a ranch cook. But if it hadn't been Jeff's idea, whose *had* it been? The question burned in her mind as the truck plummeted toward a mirage of outbuildings that seemed to float in a lake of heat.

When Jeff pulled the Bronco into the circular driveway in front of a huge ranch house—a magnificent structure of rough-hewn logs and fieldstone—he said, "Mrs. Kensington, I have to ask you something. Have you ever cooked for forty workingmen before?" She answered that she had, in fact, cooked for large groups of people on various occasions—church camp once and several times for her daughter's Girl Scout troop. Then there were the political dinners Kenneth hosted . . . Jeff Granger laughed abruptly. "This is not suburban Massachusetts, Mrs. Kensington," he said. She didn't care for his tone. Surely she had been mistaken about the "magnetic" attraction she had experienced back at the airport. It must have been the heat, the unfamiliar surroundings, the strain of travel, and her exaggerated sense of high expectations no doubt induced by fatigue. What a fool she'd been! A sudden deflation of spirit overwhelmed her. Perhaps she'd made a terrible mistake in coming here to this godforsaken place. What had made her think, after all, that her life as the accommodating wife of a minor political functionary was something to *scorn*? What had made her think that she was unusual, that she deserved something better than ninety percent of the women she knew? Why had she aspired to some lofty goal that even now she could not fully define? Jeff Granger had laughed at her, and now she laughed at herself. What had made her believe she had been given the ability to see things for what they were? She wanted to tell Jeff to turn the Bronco around, take her back to the airport. But then, where could she go? She'd burned her bridges rather thoroughly. Even if she had the capacity to humble herself before Kenneth, why should he take her back after the devastating things she'd said to him? In a cold, analytical way, she'd told him how she'd come to scorn him as a man, in his public life and in his private life as husband, father, and lover. "Christ, you even take an opinion poll in bed!" she'd told him. No, there was no way she could return to Kenneth. She'd take this job at the Y Bar Y and she'd *succeed*. If there was one virtue she possessed, it was determination. Even though Jeff Granger evidently thought very little of her, cooking for forty workingmen could not be all that different from cooking for a Girl Scout troop or for a house full of greedy politicos. It would be hard at first, even scary, but everything worthwhile in life required risk. Safety and comfort were highly overrated as far as Marianna was concerned.

She'd walked away from a twenty-year marriage without regret. The children were grown and gone. She still had time to find out who Marianna Kensington was. Perhaps she was no one. How frightening! But how much more frightening to deceive yourself into thinking you were complete when in fact you were nothing but a blank page waiting to be filled in! The suburbs were crowded with safe and comfortable women who were essentially blank pages waiting for a violating pen. Silence was their chief enemy. For silence could let the inner emptiness rise to the surface, like a submerged but featureless continent. Given an opportunity, silence would enter the house and sit down like a bold intruder. The intruder smiles with his superior knowledge of the little dark mechanisms of your heart. You pick up the latest Silhouette or Harlequin and try to read, but the words blur together, passion links arms with despair—jealousy, anger, spite, kink up like a bicycle chain that throws itself loose from its sprocket and the whole enterprise coasts to a dismal stop halfway to nowhere. You skip ahead. It doesn't help. Silence slips into the bloated prose. It invades each trumped-up scene. It collects in the gaps between chapters. It waits for you at the end in the gritty dead-white paper, rustling patiently with the last word.

The Y Bar Y was all she expected and more. From the center of the huge house a stone chimney rose massive and tall. The house itself seemed anchored to the world by the girth and heft of this proud tower. Marianna knew, then, that her decision to stay had been correct after all. There was a "rightness" in the scene that defied rational expression. Some things you know only in your heart of hearts. No logic can deny such knowledge. She was shown to her quarters—a spacious second-story room with a view of the magnificent Sangre de Cristo mountains, whose snow-capped em-

inence seemed Tibetan. Yes, yes, she *had* come to the right place
at the right time in her life. She knew it now as well as she knew
anything. It was here she would make her stand. It was here that
she would reestablish herself in the world. She shuddered, not in
trepidation, but in joyful anticipation.

When she had finished unpacking, there was a knock on the door.
It was Jeff Granger. Though she had opened the door wide, inviting
him in, he remained beyond the threshold. "Please come in," she
laughed. "I don't bite, honestly!" Jeff filled the entire doorway.
Both his shoulders grazed the frame, and his head almost touched
the top. She hadn't realized before how really large Jeff was. He
smiled—shyly, Marianna thought—and once again she felt her
heart surge with strange voltage. His smile, set against an angular
suntanned face, sent ripples of nervous spasms along her thighs
and stomach. She folded her arms across her breasts to prevent
herself from shaking visibly. She felt giddy. She didn't trust herself
to speak. "I just came by to tell you that we get off to a pretty
early start, Mrs. Kensington. So, I reckon—" Marianna interrupted
him. "Please," she said, "call me Marianna. Mrs. Kensington is
someone I am trying desperately to forget." Jeff looked at her for
a long moment. Then he said, "Marianna," as if tasting the syllables. "I like that. My mother's name is Marianne." He cleared
his throat self-consciously, as though he'd revealed something a bit
too personal about himself. "Anyway, Mrs. Ken—I mean, Marianna, the kitchen crew starts at three-thirty a.m. The men eat at
five o'clock sharp. Not a minute later. So you'd better turn in pretty
early tonight." He turned to leave, then stopped. "One other thing,
Marianna," he said, his back still turned to her. "The kitchen here
looks more like a boiler factory than any kitchen you're used to.
I suggest you let Jorge give you a run-through this evening sometime." Marianna thought, once again, that she detected a coolness
in his tone. No, she told herself, it had not been Jeff Granger's idea
to hire a woman from the East to run the kitchen of the Y Bar Y.
Before he left her room, she said, "Jeff—be honest. Just whose idea
was it to hire me, anyway? It wasn't yours, was it?" He turned to
look at her then. She saw something in his eyes that disturbed her.

Sadness? Resentment? "No," he said, slowly. "It wasn't my idea. It was my brother Thorne's idea. Thorne thought bringing in a woman from the East would give the place some . . . *class*, I think he called it." He left then, his boots echoing through the hallway and stairwell, leaving Marianna to stare at the large space he'd filled. She hadn't liked the emphasis he'd placed on "class," and yet she couldn't help but feel that Jeff Granger liked her, in spite of his obvious prejudice . . .

. . . for if this was not meant to be, then nothing was meant to be. Sometimes strangers feel they've known each other forever. Jeff was such a man to Marianna. She quivered. Passion stirred her neglected loins. Was he the man she'd envisioned? Was he her type? What was one's "type"? She had no idea. Years of careful emotions had dulled her. To know one's type is to know one's needs. Marianna was a desert of unknown needs that any random flood might violate into bloom . . .

The huge ranch-house kitchen should have been a bedlam of activity. It wasn't. The bedlam was in her mind only. There were twelve dozen eggs and eighteen pounds of bacon to fry! There were loaves and loaves of bread to toast! Gallons of coffee to make! Tubs of hash browns! Hot gravy from last night's ham drippings needed to be prepared! Marianna had help, of course, but the kitchen workers seemed reluctant to do anything without explicit instructions from her. They stood waiting—sullenly, she thought— for her to give commands. And yet they knew what they had to do—they'd been doing it all along! Clearly, she was resented here and the kitchen crew was letting her know it. Jorge Méndez, somehow, was at the root of the problem. He was her assistant, second in command, and yet he seemed as reluctant to help her as any of the underlings. She would ask him a question and he would stare at her as if it were the stupidest thing he'd ever heard. Then he'd answer slowly, enunciating the syllables as if he were speaking to a mental defective. The previous evening, when he'd given her a tour of the kitchen, he had glossed over the details of equipment operation, scheduling, duty assignments, and so on, so that she

had had to ask the same questions several times before she understood the answers. It was infuriating, and yet she did not show her
impatience. She was determined to win Jorge Méndez over to her
side, to prove to him that she was going to be a fair and loyal
supervisor, and that as far as she was concerned, his job was secure
at the Y Bar Y. Marianna was a quick learner, however, and despite
these roadblocks she managed to get breakfast served right on time,
at 5 a.m. sharp. Even though some of the eggs were fried too hard,
or some rashers of bacon too crisp, the food was more than just
edible. Lunch was no problem, since it was the function of the
chuck-wagon crew. The chuck wagon was a Mercedes-Benz diesel
bus that had been converted to hold a portable kitchen. A separate
crew ran the chuck wagon. Marianna's only responsibility regarding the lunch crew was to make sure there were enough supplies
on hand to stock the chuck wagon's refrigerators. But the evening
meal—supper—was an out-and-out disaster. At 4 p.m. Jorge Méndez wheeled a side of beef out of the cold locker and, with the help
of two kitchen boys, hoisted it onto a massive butcher-block table.
"What am I supposed to do with this?" Marianna asked. The huge,
purplish-red carcass disgusted her. "Take the rib steaks and the T-
bones, *señora*," Jorge said. "Leave the sirloin for Sunday." He
handed her a meat cleaver that must have weighed six or seven
pounds. "Make sure, *señora*, that the cuts are even—twelve to
fourteen ounces each—the *vaqueros* don't like to see a bigger piece
of meat on the plate next to them. They like it even Steven." He
left her then with the half-beef, a mountain of flesh that probably
weighed two or three hundred pounds. Marianna had two hours
to hack it into perfect steaks! In desperation she attacked the animal
with the heavy cleaver. But she struck it a glancing blow that only
gouged a wedge of fat and gristle from it. She tried again, harder,
but she hit it another off-line blow and a shrapnel of bone bits
sprayed across the kitchen. She thought she saw one of the kitchen
boys smile briefly, then turn his laughing face away from her. Jorge
Méndez returned with a big meat saw. "Perhaps if you cut away
from the shoulder back to the center loin, then with a knife you
could take it from the brisket and flank. After that it will be easy
to make your cuts. Then from the sirloin you can take flat-bone

cuts and wedge-bone cuts." His instructions meant nothing to her! She made him repeat it carefully, but now she had begun to panic and it made even less sense to her! After a half hour of sawing and hacking, the intransigent beef retained its steaks. Marianna began to cry. In that huge mass of animal flesh, there were dozens of steaks—rib-eye steaks, porterhouse steaks, club steaks, sirloins— but they would not yield themselves to her amateurish hacking. Finally, after nearly two hours of futile mutilation, she managed to produce lumps of meat that looked somewhat like beefsteaks. But there were only enough for half the men. She cut what she had into pieces the size of a large man's thumbs. These she fried on the big griddle in heavy grease. Then she ordered—too sharply, to her dismay!—one of the Mexican kitchen boys to slice twenty pounds of potatoes. The boy's eyes widened, as if she'd slapped his face, and she immediately apologized to him. He said something in Spanish and she realized that he could not understand her! New tears streamed down her face as she showed him what she wanted in a jerkily hysterical sign language. The boy cut the potatoes too thin and when she fried them in the hot grease they immediately blackened. For a vegetable she opened twenty-seven cans of asparagus and heated them to pulp in a big kettle of boiling water. When the meal was served, the cowboys would not eat it. Trays of untouched food were returned to the kitchen. "They will not eat," Jorge Méndez said, the light in his inscrutable eyes clearly triumphant. Marianna threw off her apron and ran out of the kitchen, sobbing. She ran away from the ranch house, through a grove of scrub pine, down a hill and to the grassy bank of a river. It was the worst moment in her life.

A lone rider followed her, though she was not aware of it. Under a sky the color and texture of hammered aluminum, she wept. The horseman walked his palomino to a point just above her on the river's edge. He looked down on her, a tight smile on his thin lips. He tied his horse to a stunted pine and approached her. She still was unconscious of his presence, her mind occupied, as it were, with the immediate disaster that threatened to turn her life toward a bleak future. She was thinking how worthless she was, and how stupidly arrogant she'd been to have believed that she could take over the kitchen duties at a serious cattle ranch! In a sudden fit of self-hatred, she pounded her fists into the loamy bank of the river. The rider knelt down beside her. "I sense you've had a bad day, Mrs. Kensington," he said. Marianna gasped in surprise. She looked up through tear-blurred eyes at a tall, dark man smiling down at her. She wiped the tears away with the back of her hand like a child and tried to compose herself, even though she could not immediately stop whimpering. The tall man looked remarkably like Jeff Granger, except that he was darker and had a thin mustache. His eyes, too, were different. They had a hard glint to them, and were set deeper in his head, making them seem shadowed with enigmatic musings. Like Jeff, this man was terribly handsome, but unlike Jeff, his chiseled features were dominated by a wry, disdainful loftiness of spirit that rose from a jaded cynicism. He had the look of a man who had seen just about everything the world had to offer and had found it wanting. A shiver of apprehension passed through Marianna so powerfully that the man noticed it. He sat down on the loam next to her and put his hand on hers. His hand was not hard and calloused like Jeff's but was soft, almost as soft as a woman's. He removed his hat, a black Stetson, and offered Marianna a cigarette, which she refused. "I am Thorne Granger," the man said. "Jeff's big brother. I'm sorry you had a rough afternoon. But, listen, it wasn't your fault, Marianna." She looked at him questioningly, wondering if he was only trying to boost her morale or if he actually meant what he said. Seeing the question in her eyes, Thorne insisted, "No, really, it *wasn't* your fault. Jorge was supposed to cut the beef. He's terribly offended, you know, that I hired you over him. He was expecting to take over as chief cook when Frank Delaney—our cook for twenty-eight years—died of acute cirrhosis. Jorge's good, but I wanted a woman's touch in the kitchen for a change. You can understand what I mean, can't you?" Marianna nodded, but his strangely mocking smile made her wonder just what it was she was assenting to. "In any case, I've disciplined Jorge. From now on he'll see to the meat cutting and any other work that requires a man's strength. I didn't hire you on as a stevedore. Your job, Marianna, is strictly supervisory. I want you to oversee food preparation only—to give it that woman's touch you just don't get with ordinary ranch cooks." He put his hand on her shoulder and squeezed it gently, as if to encourage her, but the pressure of his fingers promptly aroused a cautionary hesitation in her heart. She looked into his hooded eyes but could not divine his intentions at all. At that moment lightning fractured the sky and hailstones began to drum the ground. Thorne Granger leaped to his feet and untied his horse. He mounted gracefully and pulled Marianna up behind him. She felt nearly weightless in his powerful grasp. Then he trotted the horse into the shelter of a copse of quaking aspen. He swung her down from the horse as though she were a rag doll. When he dismounted, he took her roughly in his arms. He pulled her close, so close that the air was crushed out of her lungs. He kissed her then, smothering her weak protest under the bristles of his mustache. She felt the same surge of electrical current she had experienced at Jeff's more gentle touch, only now the power of it was magnified a thousand times. "You are indeed very beautiful, Marianna," he said, hoarse with contained passion. "Beauty is the only thing in the world I have respect for any longer. The rest of it can burn in Hades!" She wanted to tell him that this was no way to show respect for a lady, but his savage mouth was on hers again and he forced her backward and down until they were lying on the soft duff beneath the blowing trees. Thorne Granger's urgent manhood throbbed primitively against her helpless thighs. "No!" she screamed at last, twisting away from him. But he caught her face in his powerful hand and kissed her once again. Then he rose away from her momentarily, regarding her with eyes that seemed both innocent and insane. Marianna was terrified—too terrified to move. He put his hands on her blouse and opened it to the waist, heedless of the flying buttons. "Good Christ Almighty!" he said, his voice hushed and trembly with the sort of reverence only the damned can feel. "They are so *exquisite*, my dear!" he managed. His tortured eyes, smoldering in their sockets like coals, slaked themselves with the beauty of her breasts as a nearby flash of lightning turned them violet in the thrashing air. In spite of herself, Marianna remembered Kenneth's torpid desire, his perfunctory lust so quickly and dispassionately spent, and she felt herself loosening under the overwhelming need of Thorne Granger. Then, as if the thunder itself had become articulate, a voice shouted, "Take your rotten hands off her, Thorne!" It was Jeff, dismounting from a roan stallion, running toward them, his face mottled with rage. Thorne got up to meet his brother's charge, but Jeff struck him on the jaw before Thorne had a chance to defend himself. Thorne got up, wobbling noticeably from the force of his brother's punch. He tried to deliver a blow but Jeff ducked it neatly and floored Thorne once again. "Get back to the house, Thorne," Jeff said. "You've blown it for sure, this time." With that, Thorne Granger, visibly diminished, got up and left. "I can't tell you how sorry I am this happened, Marianna," Jeff said. Marianna pulled her shredded blouse around her exposed breasts as best she could. "He almost raped me," she said. "It's his way," Jeff replied helplessly. "Thank you," she said, "for coming when you did. I . . . didn't—" She couldn't finish. A weakness swept over her and she staggered. Jeff caught her before she fell. "I'm going to take you back to the house, Marianna," he said, picking her up in his powerful arms. "You've been through quite an ordeal. I only hope you can forgive us."

("Dear Diary: I walked away from a twenty-year marriage without regret. My kids were grown up by then and gone. I felt, and *still* feel, I had time to find out just who Marianna Kensington is. Maybe I am no one! SCARY! But how much scarier to trick yourself into thinking you are perfectly fine . . . a complete human being! Where I came from everyone thinks they are just fine. No problems. But they are just blank pages waiting for somebody to write on them. You know what they hate most? A quiet afternoon by themselves. Because the quiet hurts. I mean, the quiet is dangerous. Like a burglar is dangerous. Or like a rapist. It is there suddenly in your living room and there's no help to be found. It gets you. It has eyes and ears. It knows a lot about you. What a complete and stupid lie your life has been up to now. Squirm, squirm. It feels like uneasiness. Maybe you go to the medicine cabinet to try some more Tranxenes. Or you pick up one of those trashy novels about this woman like yourself who goes out into the world to escape from her life and gets herself into one scrape after another until Mister Right gets into her pants. Jesus, I'd rather eat bloated trash fish dredged up from Boston Harbor! It would be less poisonous to the soul. And it doesn't hold back the quiet afternoon. The quiet is there in the stupid love scenes. The quiet is there, untouched, cover to cover.")

"I only hope you can forgive us," Jeff repeated. But it wasn't really a matter of forgiveness. Marianna didn't know if she could trust Thorne Granger ever again, much less forgive him. And the most important consideration was not even Thorne Granger, but her job and her new life. What was to become of her now? She could turn tail and run back to the safety of the East, or she could grit her teeth and stick this job out. She could fight for the respect of the kitchen crew and especially for the respect of Jorge Méndez. She could do everything in her power to see that Jorge was recognized as her equal in the kitchen. And if Thorne Granger ever touched her again, or so much as looked at her offensively, she could threaten him with legal action. Women these days did not have to put up with that sort of sexual intimidation from their employers. More than anything, she did not want to fail! She wanted badly to become a first-rate professional ranch cook. *That*, she knew, was how one found oneself in this life. *That* was how one filled in the awful blanks of a blank existence. You did a job, any job, and you did it with dedication and to the best of your ability. You committed yourself. Talent was not a factor. You found the thing you did best and you did it as best you could. No job was menial or less important than any other job. Only the quality of workmanship could be assigned these arbitrary values. An inferior neurosurgeon was a "menial" compared with a prideful auto mechanic or legal secretary. She had never before grasped the simple truth of this universal fact of life. Later that evening she made a crude sign with notepaper and an India ink marking pen: I AM WHAT I DO. NO MAN CAN PROVIDE MY IDENTITY. She slept well that night, knowing that in the morning she would wake to that sign, taped to her wall, and that its wisdom would let her approach the new day with self-confidence and courage. Jorge Méndez, whether he knew it or not, had himself a damned good kitchen boss.

Before the month was out, Marianna had the kitchen under control. She'd talked to Jorge several times to clarify their relationship and to assure him that, as far as she was concerned, he was every bit as important as she was. "You will be the *corazón* of this kitchen, Jorge," she'd said, "and I will be its *alma*." This delighted Jorge. The "heart" and the "soul" of the kitchen would work together in preparing the best ranch cuisine in the West! Marianna studied Spanish every night for an hour in her room and soon was able to utter phrases in dialect that shocked the kitchen boys into gales of approving laughter. "¡*Qué la chingada*!" she would shout at minor accidents and setbacks, and the boys would whoop in delight at the immense obscenity. Jorge, as he grew to trust and respect Marianna, became her good friend. Sometimes, in moments of slack activity, they would take their coffee out to the back patio and share opinions about ranch life and life in general. She discovered that Jorge was a man of subtle intelligence and strong feelings. He had been devastated by Thorne Granger's thoughtless, even perverse, hiring of a woman with essentially no experience to supervise the kitchen. But Marianna was not about to let the injustice continue or to allow the prejudice against a *gringa* go unchallenged. She saw to it that everything done in the kitchen required Jorge's approval. And, in accepting this responsibility, Jorge became a force to contend with. His demeanor became casual and self-confident; his courtly deference was replaced by a polite assertiveness that sometimes—to Marianna's delight—furrowed the brow of Thorne Granger with confusion and, possibly, *fear*. Once, when Thorne had entered the kitchen on what was ostensibly an inspection tour, he found Jorge sitting at a table reading *The Wall Street Journal* while Marianna mixed piecrusts. Thorne had stared speechless at Jorge, but Jorge merely looked up from his paper and said, "Beef futures opened very high today, Boss." Thorne turned pale but could only say, "*Really.*" Marianna laughed, remembering the incident. She was in her room, studying her Spanish text. "¿*Qué es un romance?*" she read aloud, as someone tapped lightly on her door. It was Jeff Granger, tall in the doorway. She called him into her room. He entered, almost reluctantly, she thought. Out on the patio, some of the cowboys were playing guitars and singing. The desert was in bloom. The air was fragrant. "Thorne's left the Y Bar Y," Jeff said. "He's going to start a new life in a San Francisco brokerage firm." Marianna didn't try to conceal her feelings. "I can't say I'm unhappy," she said. But it soon became clear to Marianna that there was more on Jeff's mind than the departure of his brother. "Marianna," he said, taking her hand, "I think I've fallen in love with you." She let him kiss her, anticipating the electrical surge, but it did not come. She ushered him to the door. "We'll talk about it, Jeff. Right now I've got to do my lesson." A few minutes later, Jorge Méndez came by. Marianna let him in and closed the door. "*Alma,*" he said, kissing her hand. "*Corazón,*" she replied, her heart suddenly racing as she felt not electricity or magnetism in his touch but *heat*, the simple and generous heat of kitchens. The melodious *gringo* guitars drew them together in a long and tender embrace, and as some cowboy sang "Blue Eyes Crying in the Rain," Marianna led Jorge to her bed.

Nothing was meant to be. Sometimes when two strangers meet, their mutual strangeness seems unbridgeable. The stocky brown man of mixed blood in her arms had initially seemed unapproachably alien to Marianna. She quivered at the bizarre unpredictability of life. Passion, long dead, rioted in her loins. No, this was definitely *not* the man she'd envisioned years ago in her adolescent daydreams! He was certainly not her *type*. But what was one's "type"? Of that, more than ever, she had no idea. Years of careful emotions had dulled her judgment. For to know one's type is to know one's needs. Marianna was a desert of unknown needs this random flood was violating, with tender but strongly fluid tillage, into bloom.

She had no regrets. The children were gone. And at least she was getting to know who Marianna Kensington was. She'd been no one, she was sure of that now. How frightening! But how much more frightening to deceive yourself into thinking you were complete when in fact you were a blank page waiting to be filled in! The suburbs were crowded with safe and comfortable women who were essentially blank pages waiting for a violating pen. Silence was their enemy. Silence let the emptiness rise to the surface like a submerged but featureless continent. Silence, given a small opportunity, would enter the house and sit down like a bold intruder. The intruder smiles with his superior knowledge of the little dark mechanisms of your heart. Ignoring him, you pick up the latest Silhouette or Harlequin Romance and try to read, but the words blur together, passion links arms with despair—jealousy, anger, spite kink up like a bicycle chain that throws itself loose from its sprocket and the whole enterprise coasts to a dismal stop halfway to nowhere. You try the good parts—it doesn't help. Silence slips into the bloated prose. It invades each trumped-up scene. It collects. It is there, smirking, when you begin, there in the middle, showing a wider grin, and it waits for you at the dead end—a *surprise* ending of dead paper, rustling with the last word.

Your Story

*T*his story happened early in the history of the human race, a few years from now. It is your story, though you may have some quibbles. It's the writer's story too, but he wants to camouflage it. (The form he's chosen confirms this.) Look at it this way: he offers a parable of a parable, nut and shell, easily cracked and eaten. But the question is, will it nourish or poison or just lie suspended in the gut like a stone? It points no finger of blame, pats no one on the back, gives no guarantees beyond asserting the commonality of its long-lost roots, which are transplantable anywhere. To make matters worse, the writer (never applauded for his penetrating insights and infamous for his lack of convictions) probably won't get it right. He'll need your open-minded help to fill in the blanks or to blank out the excesses. Excess is his forte. He's made a tidy little career of it. Actually, he'll need more than your help, but nothing can be done about *that*. The narcissistic dissembler is on his own:

There once were a husband and wife who were so simple that they had no control over their lives or the lives of their children. Worse, they had no control over what they said. Words gushed out of her mouth like blood from a bad gash—hot, pure, terrible to behold. From his mouth they were like the dark, sour smoke from a doused fire. The two of them were reasonably civilized. They were respected in their community. Their names were ordinary: Gene and Amy Underhill. Names like these do not arouse suspicion or resentment.

One evening, at the dinner table, Amy said to Gene, "Honey, I want to get rid of the children. I've had enough of them. I want to get rid of them tomorrow."

This wasn't the first time Amy had expressed this wish. She was not one to mince words, but this was the first time she'd set a deadline.

"Well, they *are* shits," Gene agreed affably. Gene Underhill was a decent, mild-mannered man who worked as a lab technician for a company that produced titanium-alloy butterfly valves for a secret defense project rumored to be linked to the "Star Wars" program. He spoke his mind freely too, but with far less heat than his wife. He was by nature a cautious, reflective man. His wife's forthright manner kept him off balance. He was no match for her, and knew it. "I don't think I'd be able to actually *harm* them, dear," he said.

Amy, whose anger was so reliable a stone church could lean against it and not topple, said, "You incredible wimp."

Gene knew there would be no lovemaking that night, or, if there was, it would be rancorous. Which in itself could be interesting. If the rancor could be harnessed and guided into some infrequently traveled byways. Images of Gortex straps with Velcro fasteners, Spandex collars, electrified quirts, suppositories dipped in non-prescription euphorics, Suggesto-Vision videotapes from the Exotica/Erotica section of the neighborhood 7-Eleven store, and so on, occurred to him.

"I read you like a book," Amy said, noticing the sweat beads forming on Gene's upper lip. "But you can put fun and games out of your mind until we get this business settled once and for all. *Then* we'll party."

Gene and Amy were eating a dinner of half-warm Big Macs and fries. The children, Buddy and Jill, had been put to bed earlier.

"We could send them away to boarding school," Gene said hopefully. He dipped his last fry into a kidney-shaped pool of catsup. He made a project out of it to avoid Amy's eyes.

"Wonderful," Amy said. "We'll send them to school in England and you and I will live in a villa on the Côte d'Azur and read French poetry and paint neo-cubist nudes. Jesus, Gene, grow *up*, will you?"

Gene and Amy were not bad people. They were beleaguered by

debts they had foolishly allowed to accumulate until, at twenty-two percent interest, the debts took on an unearthly life of their own and became a fiscal Frankenstein monster that sought to destroy its creators. Gene and Amy were harassed daily by the thousand large and small demands of an underfunded, barely marginal, middle-class life-style. Every night they were afflicted by televised world events whose increasingly inventive perversities left them confused, angry, and spiritually at sea. The children, typically, were whiny ingrates who rarely rewarded their parents with a hint of promise, academic or otherwise. "You are a slob, just like your father," Amy once said to Buddy, in a fit of rage. Jill, on the other hand, filled Amy with silent dread. Her daughter was a miniature of herself, a brooding waxen doll. Sometimes she would catch Jill studying her with eyes that were too knowledgeable. Those dark eyes always seemed judgmental and full of sad reproach. She felt accused of some nameless crime by those eyes and was moved, frequently, to defend herself to her own daughter. It didn't make sense, but there it was, the heavy load of guilt. Amy once screamed, "I don't *deserve* this! I haven't done anything to you!" but knew, instinctively, it sounded not only crazy but *false*.

"All right," Gene said at last. "We'll do it." He felt old and heavy. He was prematurely gray and the smile lines around his eyes and mouth had hardened into permanent fissures that gave him the appearance of constant flinching. He was surprised daily by this face of his in the shaving mirror. He was only forty but he looked sixty. And yet he felt no different than he did when he was twenty. The mental picture he carried of himself was of a dark-haired, smooth-skinned boy with a good-natured smile. How had this happened? The last french fry he'd eaten had lodged itself in his chest, under his breastbone, where it scratched at him like a greasy, long-nailed finger. "We'll do it tomorrow," he said. "First thing after breakfast."

Amy got up and kissed him. "I'm so relieved, darling," she said.

Which means . . . Gene remarked hopefully to himself, new sweat beads glazing his lip . . .

"I'm in the moo-ood," Amy crooned, completing his thought.

They went up to bed. Amy was happy now. Soon, she felt, her

problems would be solved. Soon, their priorities would be reordered and they would be able to concentrate on getting out of debt. Amy was only thirty-three years old and had seen enough of empty cupboards and overdrawn checking accounts and her daughter's accusing eyes. She wanted a secure, predictable life. She wanted to devote most of her time to income management, the search for safe investments, and to the establishment of a first-rate Individual Retirement Account. And she wanted to do this without *guilt*, or any other distraction.

Amy undressed slowly in the dim bedroom, revealing in tantalizing increments her still lovely body to her eager husband. Gene was already in bed, the chalk of liquid Maalox caking his lips. "Gortex straps," he suggested, hoarse with emotion.

"All right," Amy agreed. "Since you've decided to face reality like a grown-up, for once."

I turned my back on them at this point and left them to their constrained pleasures. I went to see the children. I danced my way down the creaky hall to their room. Left foot over right, hop and skip, right foot over left, turn and turn. Among other things, I am a dancer.

The children, never quite as stupid or indifferent as their parents believe, had heard it all. They were frightened, but not especially surprised.

"What will we *do*?" Jill asked her brother, Buddy.

"Play it dumb, like always," Buddy said.

Jill was nine and Buddy was going on twelve. They were beautiful children, blond as late summer wheat. They were tucked in their beds, the girl on one side of the room, the boy on the other. I kissed the girl and then the boy. The pages of the boy's comic book were riffled, as if by wind. I turned in slow, elegant circles between their sweet beds, but they saw only the shadows of their dreams.

The next day was Sunday. The family set out for the woods ostensibly to gather firewood for the coming fall. The children rode in the back of the pickup truck along with the chain saws and gas cans. It was a beautiful morning, cool and clear.

After Gene had turned off the main highway and had entered a narrow dirt road that led to the wooded foothills, Amy said, "Once we get into the trees, get off the road."

Gene slipped the Toyota into four-wheel drive, anticipating a rough climb. He leaned his head out the window and yelled back to the kids. "Hang on tight," he said. "Don't try to stand up or anything."

The engine labored as the truck struggled against the steep, loamy-ground of the forest. "Keep switching back and forth," Amy said. "I want them to lose all sense of direction."

They traveled this way for nearly an hour. Gene, holding the wheel so tightly his hands were cramped and white, was sweating profusely. He was relieved when he found a dry creek bed that led out into a meadow. He accelerated through the wide field, which glowed almost unnaturally, like the core of a nuclear reactor, with wild flowers. He stopped in the middle of this exotic place and unscrewed the thermos. He took a long drink of whiskied coffee. "I'm lost," he said.

"Good," said Amy. "Keep driving."

On the other side of the meadow, the mountains began. Gene found an old logging road. It was very steep and he had to keep the Toyota in its lowest gear to manage the climb. Their ears popped and the air became noticeably cooler. The silver-gray stumps of ancient clear-cuts studded the steep slopes like rooted tables. Patches of snow between the great stumps looked like dropped linen. The air was purer here and the sky was so blue it seemed like the inside of an enameled egg.

They entered an area of standing-dead trees. "Good pickings," Gene said, stopping the truck and setting the brake.

"Keep going," Amy said. "We didn't come all the way up here for firewood, damn it."

Gene sighed and restarted the engine. They drove for another hour, passing more groves of dead trees, slash piles, and old, abandoned logs that sawyers had left behind for unknown reasons. The sun was low and smoky in the sky. The children, cold and hungry, were whining and tapping on the rear window of the truck cab. "We're almost there!" Amy yelled through the glass.

Gene looked at his wife. There was something in her face he had never noticed before but would always see from this day on. If he had to name it he would call it "grim determination," but even this description seemed to fall short. Amy was an attractive woman, but the set of the jaw and the cast of her eyes undercut her beauty. It was as if another Amy, the "real" Amy Underhill, had surfaced at last. Gene felt a sinking sensation in his abdomen, which he misconstrued as excitement.

When they were at an altitude where only stunted dwarf trees grew, they stopped and got out of the truck. There were a few beetle-killed trees, none of them more than twelve feet tall, on the upslope side of the truck. Gene went after these with the smaller of his saws. Amy took the children for a walk to gather berries. She herded them across screes of unstable shale, through thick, angry patches of scrub pine, across snowfields, and, finally, to a sheltered area where an abundance of huckleberry bushes grew. She gave the children a large plastic bag each. "Fill them with berries," she said, "while daddy cuts a load of wood. Then we'll go into town and eat at McDonald's. You'll have a real appetite by then."

She walked swiftly back to the truck, which was half loaded with firewood. "Shut off that saw and let's go!" she yelled at Gene, who was about to fell another dwarf tree.

Gene switched off his saw. "Hey, no sense in going back with half a load," he said, grinning sheepishly. She still had that look on her face, the look that made him believe no one ever knows the person they live with, and that nothing in the world is constant.

"Don't play for time. It won't work. We're going through with this, Gene."

"Whatever," Gene said, realizing that he could not match her resolve. He started the truck, hoping the children would not hear it, then hoping they would. "We are pretty darned evil," he said, mostly to himself.

"Uh-huh," Amy answered. "We're real novelties."

"But people just do not abandon their kids in the mountains!"

Amy didn't respond to this outburst. How could she respond to a silly remark that represented, so unconditionally, the generic pudding that served as her husband's brain?

I left them just as Gene was about to notice that Amy had changed again, and not just in her expression. She seemed *physically* different now. The bridge of her nose, for example, was beaky and shinier than before, her lips thinner, the angular jut of her jaw more acute, her tall forehead striated with astonishing areas of depleted pigments. He would tell himself (what choice did he have?) that these were only shades of difference that he might have noticed earlier had he been more attentive—people do change, after all— but this threadbare argument would be shredded before the honest rage of his nightmares.

I oared into the sky on my glossy black wings and sailed toward the children. They hadn't heard the truck start and were still picking berries. I watched them from a majestic altitude, enjoying the thermals, the heckling squadrons of starlings, and the unmatched beauty of the northern forests.

By the time their plastic bags were nearly filled with the dark red berries, the sun had slipped below the horizon. The cold mountain air crept out of the shadows, where it had survived the day, to reclaim the evening and coming night. "We'd better head back to the truck," Buddy said, looking up into the deepening sky, where the brightest stars were already twinkling.

But the long shadows the mountain put down obscured the trail. When they arrived at the steep scree of shale it was too dark to find the path that crossed it. And as Buddy stepped out onto the precarious slope of loose rock, he started a small landslide. The lonely echo of clattering rocks made Jill whimper. Buddy scrambled back to safety.

"What are we going to *do?*" Jill cried.

Now an ambassadorial bear with cubs, I ambled out of some huckleberry bushes behind the children, my long, red mouth dripping with my favorite fruit. My two cubs rollicked alongside.

"Oh no!" Jill cried. "It's a bear!"

"Don't move," Buddy said. "They can't see very well. Maybe she hasn't noticed us."

"Don't be afraid, children," I said, sweetly as my crude vocal cords would allow. I stopped directly in front of them and rolled on my back. My playful cubs pounced on me and bit my furry breasts. I slapped them away and growled, startled somewhat by the aggression of the little beasties, then gathered them up in my arms and we rolled together through thick spears of bear grass, chuffing and moaning with bear-family pleasure.

The boy hugged his little sister protectively. In the dying light their pale faces glowed supernaturally. Bears can see these auras; most humans cannot. "Follow me, children," I said. I turned from them and ambled away, downslope, into the thicket below.

It was almost dark by the time they arrived at my house. I vanished into my own shadow and watched them from several vantage points at once. What fine, holy animals they were!

"What is that?" the girl asked her brother.

"A house," he said. "A funny-looking little old house."

They came closer, close enough to reach out and touch the delicious walls. "I think it's made out of food," the boy said, licking his sticky fingers.

"Cake!" shrieked the girl. "It's a cake house!"

They pushed open the hard marzipan door and entered. I was seated at the table in a more customary form. "Good evening, little ones," I said, my ancient voice scratchy and dry.

The girl screamed and the boy picked up a piece of firewood, which he held in both hands as a weapon.

"There's nothing to be afraid of, children," I said, smiling.

"It's a witch!" cried the girl. "A horrible old witch with dead gray teeth!"

"Let's go," the boy said, pulling his transfixed sister toward the door.

"You must stay at least for supper," I said.

Because they were very hungry by now, they approached the table but took seats at the opposite end. I smiled at their caution. "Too much caution can become a bad habit, my dears," I said, though they could not understand the significance of my words. I changed the subject. "Let's play a game, children."

"First we eat," said the boy. He was a hardheaded little rascal who appeared far brighter and more sure of himself than his slip-shod, weak-willed father.

I set a good table of venison, broiled grayling, wild asparagus, goat's milk, sunflower bread with dandelion honey. They ate like little pigs. Their naïve unchecked appetite made my heart expand. Too soon they would be concerned with calorie counting, cholesterol content, and all the other drivel that makes the alimentary canal a quivering battleground of false causes.

When they finished this fine meal, they sighed in real contentment and gratitude. "You're welcome," I said, not in rebuke but in response to their little burps and the slack-jawed trance of happy satiation.

The girl became drowsy and fell asleep at the table. I carried her to a bedroom I had prepared in advance. When I rejoined the boy, he said, "Jill's had a hard couple of days, ma'am." His eyes held mine and did not blink. I liked him. He seemed to grow more mature by the minute. He would do well in the difficult world ahead.

"How about you?" I said. "Are you ready for a little game? You might win a nice prize."

"Sure," he said. His trust was edged with a steely-eyed wariness, but he was not one to play it safe, knowing instinctively that the only real way to lose was to not play at all.

"Then come with me. I'll show you something you won't forget."

I took him out to my barn. "Where are the animals?" he asked. I held up my stick and pointed upward. "Hey, there's no *roof* on this barn. How come?"

"To let the starlight in," I said. I touched his shoulder with my stick. He jumped straight up as if I'd given him an electric shock.

"What's that music?" he asked.

"Stars," I said. "They sing on long wires of light. Listen." What the boy heard was this:

> only the child
> can see the hand
> that made the wild
> mysterious land

I touched his other shoulder with my stick and he jumped again. When he came down he landed on his hands and knees. "Enjoy yourself," I said. "I'll be back for you later."

The boy had jumped the line that separates human folly from the natural order, and he was at that moment running through the woods on all fours with a pack of wolves. He ran and ran, chasing the hart, feeling the joy of speed and strength, the comfort of the tribe and the unchecked lust of the hunt. When he grew tired he returned to his slumber, then woke to the music of the stars, which he would forget only at his peril.

The next morning the girl demanded to know what I'd done with her brother.

"He's been playing a game," I said.

"You lie," she said, stern as her mother.

I gave her a witchy smile, sinister and cunning. "Help me clean this house, you snot," I said.

My profound ugliness intimidated her. She picked up a broom. Then, as was customary, I made what all the children see as my fatal mistake. I bent over next to the open door of my oven, pretending to scour a spot of grease from the floor, and waited for the blow. She delivered it on schedule. The broom whacked me across my bony old buttocks and I obliged her by falling headfirst into the oven. For effect, I let loose a blood-chilling scream of vile curses that antedate the development of speech organs in the so-called *Homo sapiens*. She slammed the iron door shut and wedged her broom handle against it so that it could not be opened. Then she turned the gas up high. I heard the pilot light ignite the ring of gas and searing heat blew up into my face.

The boy entered the house then. He was still groggy from his hard sleep and was trying to adjust the vagrant grammar of his dreams to the tight parsings of authorized reality. When he understood what his sister had done, he became upset. "She didn't mean us any harm, Jill," he said.

"Yes, she did!" Jill cried out, wounded by Buddy's ingratitude. She had saved them, hadn't she, from the witch's evil schemes?

Buddy noticed the Polaroids I had taken of them while they

slept. I'd tacked them up on the wall. He went to the pictures and stared at the angelic towheads, who resembled their parents only superficially. "See," he said, "she liked us well enough to take our pictures, Jill."

"What's that *smell*?" Jill asked, her eyes widening in delight.

The house was filling with a fragrance that was so sweet, so tempting, that their mouths began to water instantly. They forgot the Polaroids, forgot their argument, and could think of nothing else except the wonderful aroma and where it might be coming from. It was coming from the oven, of course, and as if to underscore this fact, the buzzing of the timer rattled the air.

The boy went to the oven and peeked in. Inside, perfectly baked, was an angel food cake. (*C'est moi.*) The boy took it out, using pot holders, and set it on the table.

"Maybe I was only dreaming about a witch," the children said in unison.

Only dreaming or, worse, *It was only a bad dream* are the formulas that have exiled me from the world for several hundred years. Children would have those scoffing catchphrases stenciled into their brains and the useful truth of their dreams would be dismissed time and again until the children grew into gray, dreamless entities of no consequence who would commit blunder after blunder on their murderously banal trip to the grave.

I suppose the story must end there, though the writer is pressing for one of his patented, neatly delivered, full-circle endings. For instance, he would like to see Buddy and Jill, older and honed to an edge by the harsh world, make their way home and confront their parents. Buddy would have a Ruger .357 magnum in his belt and Jill's purse would be stocked with street drugs. (The writer has other murky ideas, generated by his need for what he thinks of as *neatness*. He calls these blind spots "satisfying endings." My motto is: Never trust an anal narcissist. The flattering mirror he cavorts in front of shows a geometrically precise world, tied up neat as a Christmas package.)

The writer would like to tell you something about me, as an object of (in this case) blame. But he hasn't understood yet the extent of my influence, the depth of my interest, or how he is my last refuge in a world that has excluded me. He is one of you, after all, no better and no worse. For example, he would like to know where I am *now*, when he needs me most. He doesn't realize that I'm always here, in his word processor, among the binary digits of the software, in the wiring and microchips, in the copper and silicon atoms, down among the leptons and quarks and gluons, and further, where time and space no longer exist, in the null of nulls, riding the crest of wave after wave of pulsing energy, a cosmic surfer, everywhere and nowhere, inside and outside, locus of a geometry of tucks and puckers. And I am in the stymied axons and dendrites of the writer's poor brain, break-dancing on the cerebral dunes as he rises from his desk and goes out to the kitchen for his twelfth cup of coffee, hoping for the final rush of syllables that chase and corner all the meanings of the story and truss them up with granny knots of inevitability. But there are large densities in the dross of his being, crazy opacities, flashes of perfect nonsense. He tries so hard, but he never says exactly what he means. (Though he means everything he says.) He is my puppet, but, alas, he is on very loose strings.

Just now, he's in his backyard sipping tequila from a flask, refusing to let the story go. He has climbed up to the top branches of his willow tree. It is a windy summer's night, and the stars are blowing through the whipping leaves like hissing, incandescent moths. "If I end it there," he complains to me, "no one will get the point!"

Let's leave him up the tree. He's not quite bright enough to trust you. Also, if we allowed him to design an ending and bandage it to the story, who's to say he wouldn't produce a monster? No. It's *your* story, reader, and you are always in the middle of it.

The Coming Triumph
of the Free World

*T*he grizzled psychotic entered Safeway laughing. His laugh had the false heartiness of a department store Santa Claus. He stood in front of the checkout lines, chuckling at some private observation that tickled him. He was full of expansive, arm-waving gestures. A young woman, on her way out, made the mistake of stopping near him to adjust the shoulder strap of her purse. He laughed out loud and opened his arms, inviting her to join his merry world. As his arm circled her neck, she pushed it deftly away, as if accustomed to handling the blunt familiarities of the insane. She was good-natured and not at all frightened. The man was at least six feet three and over two hundred pounds. His raggy clothes were leathery with hardened filth.

I'd seen him before. He was not usually so happy. Most of the time he seemed stunned and bewildered. He'd stand, teetering on the balls of his feet, touching his face with trembling fingertips as if trying to remember how it once looked. Or he would move, zombie-slow, through the aisles, perplexed by the rage of colors and shapes that gleamed like hallucinations from the shelves. Once I saw him marching fiercely to a Sousa piece on the Muzak, a large fresh salmon and a six-pack of toilet paper in his cart. I didn't know his name, but I called him Muni, after the 1930s movie actor Paul Muni, whom the man resembled in some distorted way.

Muni followed the young woman out of the store and into the moonlit parking lot. A checkout clerk followed them to make sure Muni didn't try any rough stuff. I wheeled my cart after the clerk, thinking that neither one of us would be a match for Muni if he got it into his head to fight for love. Raquel, my wife, lagged at the checkout counter, squinting suspiciously at the receipt. "Are you coming?" I yelled. I was nervous and annoyed. Muni wasn't the only reason for getting out of Safeway quickly. They were out in droves that Monday night, even though the moon was not quite full . . . bag ladies, bikers, frayed winos fondling slim bottles of fortified Tokay. A tall, reeling Indian had stopped us several times. He'd wanted advice on certain items. It was a transparent ploy. What he really wanted was social contact. "Don't *talk* to him," Raquel said. But I couldn't help myself. We're social animals, and I responded to the gesture we all must respond to or give up entirely our mostly bogus claim to community.

"So, what do you think about these Cocoa Puffs?" he'd asked me.

"Empty calories," I said. "Don't waste your money."

Far away, I heard Raquel say, "*Estúpido,*" in steamy Hispanic syllables.

"Generic cornflakes are your best buy," I said.

"So, generic cornflakes, you say," he said, scratching his sparsely whiskered chin thoughtfully.

The antidepressants I'd been taking made me thirsty most of the time, and so I went to the soft-drink cooler and popped open a Diet Pepsi. Raquel, from a distance, saw me do this. She put her hands on her hips and scowled. The Indian had followed me to the cooler. "Tell me seriously," he said, his sweet wine breath dilating the air between us. "Do they still make Cliquot Club?"

Out in the parking lot, Muni was leaning into the young woman's Jeep. The clerk who had gone out to protect her was keeping his distance. He was frowning, arms folded sternly across his apron. He obviously lived in a neighborhood where such gestures have impact. Here, in the low-rent section of town, they were invisible. The young woman, though, was in control of the situation. She pushed Muni's wild head out of her window and started the Jeep. Muni was still laughing like a paid Santa, and the girl was laughing too. She had thrilled him by putting her good-natured hand on his unwanted head and shoving it away. It was rejection, but there was compassion in it. It was the best Muni could hope for.

"Christ," Raquel snorted as I backed our old Datsun out of the parking slot. "Why do we *come* to this godforsaken place?"

"The pasta," I reminded her. It was the one store in town that carried a good, cheap durum semolina. Since I was doing the cooking these days, I insisted on it.

I'd been out of work for six months. Raquel had taken a job with the city and was learning how to program an IBM. She hated computers, had a superstitious fear of them, and now, here she was, processing words for the Department of Streets. She was tired and short-tempered most of the time. Her lovely eyes were red with fatigue. She went to bed early, as usual, and I watched TV.

I watched a football game that had more beer commercials than running plays. "Guys, it doesn't get any better than this," said a maudlin canoeist in one of the commercials. Then I watched an entire James Bond movie, Sean Connery having sport with several gleaming creatures between bizarre attempts on his life. His wars were often fought in the Bahamas, as if the coming triumph of the free world were tied, somehow, to white sand, blue water, and submarine sex. "Compassion is your fatal weakness, James," said the gleaming counterspy under 007.

I watched a pair of lumbering white heavyweights hammer each other into early senility on the Sports Channel, then went up to bed. Raquel was snoring lightly. I kissed her long, salty back, but she did not stir.

In my first dream, Muni and I were in the Bahamas, gazing out at a flotilla of sinister yachts. Muni was still laughing, but with failing heartiness. Then *I* was Muni, helmeted in his skull. A spectacular urge to laugh wrenched me out of the dream and I woke up laughing. I rolled out of bed and stumbled across the dark bedroom, laughing. Raquel, her resolute back still turned, said, "What? What is it?"

I had no specific answer.

I could only touch my face with trembling fingertips as the black world around me, yoked to a rhythm it could neither escape nor follow, reeled helplessly by.

The Swimmer
in Hard Light

The woman in my best painting—picture Soutine's lonely nude, the meat-faced woman with red knuckles—has lost her two children to the lake. The lake isn't in the scene. Maybe it will be later. There's no sign of the kids, either. Twin boys. Somebody who won't give his name is standing a little to one side and a step behind the woman on the wet planks of the boat ramp. He's saying something to her, saying that he'll swim out to them, promising to retrieve the lost babies. It's a promise he won't be able to keep. I know it, you know it, but we are seeing him when he believed in himself absolutely. Unlike him, we have the privilege of perspective. The concept is easily my best, even though it's off to a shaky start.

The boating accident on Blue Lake—you remember? That's what I'm talking about. It was in the papers. "Mere words cannot express my profound sorrow," said the Mayor. The rhetoric of high office—how impossible to escape it, even here. The woman squats on the ramp in ankle-deep water (remember the human-interest Wirephoto?), clutching her breasts as if the blame were somehow in them. Could you stand it? Did some small part of your heart lose oxygen and die? Did you turn to the mercy of the Sports Section as fast as you could?

The woman in my canvas, though, is clutching a black guitar, her long, oversucked breasts resting on the cold ebony. I'm looking for Edward Hopper's sense of the *thing*. How the *thing* exists for itself and itself alone. How it steals the scene. How it produces instant feelings of irrelevance in the viewer. A world of unmoving solids has no place in it for that drifter, the soul. Hopper is one of the dangerous ones. (Countertop café pie can leave you feeling abandoned. Curtains blowing in a dark hotel window will give you bad dreams. A gas station in Iowa can stun you to your knees.) Hopper eliminated time from the world of solids, kept only space. He put us in zombie-land.

My woman is singing, there on the ramp. The humpback clouds on the close horizon will remind you of body bags. There is an Oriental wind chime tinkling. Her clothes are institutional gray. But she is lovely withal, caught between seeing and not seeing, between looking and turning away. You can take these rare moments from coarse, inhuman paint. If you're lucky enough.

I try to paint only when the light can't dominate. The morning hours, between six and nine, when the light is still rock-hard. Later than that and the grays soften into lead or silver, the blues turn nobly Scandinavian, bone-elegant white softens into wholesome cream. This is southwestern America, 1975, suited only to convalescence and detention. (I qualify for both.) The local Indians tricked mystic siennas out of this burning sky, but we are not the Indians. Color becomes richly medicinal here as the sun climbs. If you are searching for something in the oils, you take the major part of the local day as false. One who has the mind of an interior decorator might give you promising psychotropic Edens. But we've had enough of that. On the other hand, never underestimate what this country will fall for.

I discovered the treachery of this local light one late morning. I felt good, starting the day. My strokes were quick and sure; I felt as if I were giving a speech before the Press Club. I was even whistling. But the painting, as it emerged before my helpless eyes, was a disaster. Even so, I couldn't stop myself. Stroke, stroke, stroke. Her mouth opened, a scream of pleasure tightened her throat, her eyes rolled back. I was painting with a hard-on—always a mistake, never mind what Picasso might have said.

I watched, helpless, as her fingers grew plump and soft, the color of standing cream, all of it suggesting the good life. Her brow bulged like a white melon, teeming with sweet, half-baked ideas. I stepped back from the mess and saw a *halo*. "*Grieve*, you grinning floozy," I told her.

The model, Miss Klein, a student from a local community college, became alarmed. I kicked the coming Madonna off her easel, stepped on the double-crossing paint, waffling the smug flesh with the zipper print of my Nikes. Miss Klein put on her shirt.

"Come back, Klein, in fifteen years!" I yelled, but it wasn't her fault. It was the *light*, the tyrannical southwestern light, but I didn't understand that yet. Later, blessed by a Canadian front, with overcast, I saw the problem.

I didn't burn the canvas, though. I needed to study the failure, to remember it. The others loved it. "Now, *that's* what I call painting, Smitty!" said the chaplain. "It gives me a lift." He handed me a chocolate ice cream cone. I shoved it into the bourgeois Madonna's lap and pumped it home. "She likes chocolate cock, Rev," I explained. The sophisticated chaplain chortled sadly. We're all shockproof these days, even the priests. Especially the priests. Nothing is profane enough, nothing blasphemous enough. The bodily humors barely raise a smile. It follows then that we have entered a new age of innocence. Our ancient power to shock each other has been canceled. We are naked again, reborn in a high-tech Eden, watched over by disinterested electronic gods.

"You're getting very very good," said the chaplain. "And I don't mean technique. You're getting beyond technique. You're saying something, Smitty."

"Thanks," I said, but he was just dazzled.

"It's clean, Smitty. You've purged all your false moves."

"Cow flop, chaplain, and you know it."

There were plenty of false moves in my paint. They were in the weight of the stroke, mix of pigment, the fullness or poverty of knuckle and breast. A fistful of false moves waited to jump out onto the canvas from their little closets. I thought of Van Gogh's ear, but it was my fine Italian hand I wanted to mutilate. Then I'd finish the painting with my foot. Maybe the wrong moves could be stopped at the hip or knee. The laboring foot would yield my Madonna.

I took dirty Polaroids of Miss Klein, but she didn't know they were dirty. (The tangy tunnel buried in the damp delta, dark channel to big thrills and bigger pain.) "Go away, Klein. Come back in twenty years." But I fell into her cheery arms and pulled at her scarless breasts with infantile concentration. "You're such a *quirky* asshole, Smitty," she said merrily.

I was taken to sick bay. Valium and Muzak for Captain Quirk: no paint allowed. "They rip you up, Smitty. You get obsessed," Doctor says. Fluorescent overheads and naked walls, the nailed-down window giving out on a view of smilax and goldenrod. I had nothing to work with. Bad luck, since the view—low gray buildings at the end of a stunning field—begged for Hopperesque renditions. I collected my semen in a juice glass and painted monochromatic landscapes on the walls, taking a bit of color from my wrist. Back to basics: finger painting with body juice. Good binding agent, jism, for the sanguine pigment.

I'm sending away for Kodachromes of the Eiffel Tower. I want to show, in the Fauvist way, a point where nationalism and art leach at each other's breasts, and how the exchange is mutually toxic. Title: *The Poisoned Tower*. An academic diversion. A little easy fun for a change. I've asked Neil Armstrong to send me a snapshot of his hand, gloved and resting on a lunar instrument. I'm going to put the Eiffel Tower in the Sea of Tranquillity. Neil will try to climb it, and fat old Earth, blue blob in the black, airless sky, will hold her breath. I didn't mention the reason I wanted his hand. We met once in Houston, and again in Washington. Nice man. Brave. But brave enough to respond to *me*? Will he take the trouble to ask, "Smitty, why my *hand*?"

When I was in government, my associates called me the Swimmer. No flap, no adverse turn of events, no administrative shake-up, no coup or loss of face could disturb the measured strokes with which I carried out the directives of the Boss. I was not exactly Cabinet level, but I answered only to the Boss himself. ("What's the word from Santiago, Smitty?" he'd ask, and I'd reply, "They're calling you Boca Loca, chief. Crazy Mouth." I was one of the few who could talk to him this way. He liked me. He thought of me as his protégé.) I mention all this to give you some idea of my former rank, how long my fall, and how I've landed on my feet even though locked up in this country club with some of the nation's finest. I wore eight-hundred-dollar suits, three-hundred-dollar shoes, my car was a stretched Caddy driven by a six-foot-seven-inch black called Wes. Then came the media event that sent us all packing, even the Boss. "Smitty, what the Christ went wrong?" he asked me. We were on our knees in the Oval Office, trying to remember a prayer. "Everything," I said. "Everything that doesn't count." My name, by the way, is not Smith. My crime was loyalty to the Boss. My crime was efficiency, pragmatism, and, worst of all, *intelligence. Machiavelli*! screamed my old friends in the press corps. Am I bitter? No. Bitterness is self-directed spite and will cause cancers to grow in the always willing garden of the body.

The Black Guitar. That's my working title for my rugged little anti-Madonna, although I do admire the simplicity of *Woman Grieving on Boat Ramp*, like an understated Hopper. (Hopper: *My Roof. House with a Big Pine. Hotel Window.* He was shrewd. He wasn't about to let *words* steal the show by using a flashy title.) I've shown my collection of Hopper prints to Miss Klein. "He gives me the heebie-jeebies," she said. She expects me to tell her how dumb she is, but instead I say, "You're right to feel that way, Miss Klein. Only dead meat wouldn't feel that way."

The mouth, though collapsing at the corners, is strong. The hands are welded to the music. The knuckles are raw and gray. The long, hard fingers scrape at the strings as if at the fresh ground above a grave. Her eyes have seen too much today and are closed. She has seen it, the dark thing that Hopper lived with, the thing that nullifies time and declares great static space as All, every cubic mile of it.

The background: a few helpless bystanders, not brave enough to try to save her babies. Trees in late-autumn sun, not quite bare, a cold house (I stole the windows from Hopper), its doors massively closed. A touch of sacrificial red blares behind the trees, suggesting the lights of an emergency vehicle.

Inspiration vs. execution. The old battle. Technically you could say it's done. But something is missing. It could be a single stroke, or it could be one stroke too many, or it could be everything. One dark line, not quite bisecting the blank canvas—that could be the whole picture, but I am no Rothko. Hopper, by expelling time, revealed the stasis. In a Hopper there is no movement, no possibility of movement. Movement can't exist even as an idea. Movement is the mother and father of time. When space is an unlimited absolute, nothing moves. Miss Klein, comfortable citizen of our kinetic democracy, senses this in Hopper and gets the heebie-jeebies.

I stare at the canvas and beyond, at my Miss Klein, who is staring at the wall clock, dreaming of Corvettes. She is from a good suburb. Even the houses there look like they are *cruising*. Life is a cruise, they seem to say. Lean joggers, our apostles of Motion, are daily reminders that to *get* anywhere, you've got to *move*. But even the Boss saw through that national hallucination. ("Smitty, it occurs to me that we aren't getting anywhere. You sense it?" We were having lunch with the Secretary of State and the Attorney General. "We need patience," said the Secretary. "Bullshit," the Boss replied. The subject was Africa or China or Central America, but it soon swerved into a general consideration of Political Life. "We're going in circles," said the Boss, orbiting one index finger with another. He winked secretly at me. I returned it with a quick wink of my own. It stayed with me, the habit, became an unstoppable twitch, leading some people to question my sincerity or stability. I am a winker, the least trusted of men.)

I tried to explain grief to Miss Klein, how abruptly physical it is, how it pops up out of nowhere when the mind had been mercifully distracted and delivers the blow that transforms the momentary illusion of freedom into a suffocating pressure. I wanted her to know the mind of my anti-Mary. But her small, unsuspecting womb is tight with piquant notions. It has channeled no darlings into the light. I requested an older woman, a pain-scarred mother of a confusing brood, a tranquilized insomniac of depth and power, but no one answered my ad.

To tease her out of boredom, I say, "Do you know yourself, Miss Klein?"

"No," she says.

In such small ways she continually redeems herself.

I touch the slippery ramp and shake the water out of my ears. I tried to save them. I did all I could. I swim well, I always did. Believe that.

But the swimmer is alive and free—good appetite, taking a steam bath from time to time, a failed Christ, lunching with Pilate now and then, good as ever in heart, but suddenly short of grace. Short of grace, out of time, belly plump with chutney and chops. Good soul, true but tired, realizing at last that we are just *here*, in a real *place*, for better or worse, forever. He reaches for the woman's shoulder, but cannot make himself touch her. "Mere words," said the Mayor, "cannot express my profound sorrow."

I feel the swimmer's desolation. Not lonely, not overwhelmed by the loss of the children (which after all is not *his* loss), and certainly not bitter over the misunderstandings, genuine and deliberate, the betrayals, or the journalistic abuse he will have to suffer for the rest of his life. Even his imprisonment (the word is an insult to hard-timers, since this is more like a religious retreat with tennis and squash than time in the Joint) will not make him bitter. He is too proud to let bitterness destroy him, and he is wary. Too proud and wary to slip into a self-righteous funk. He will swim, he will continue to swim, in the Sea of Dead Hope. See him out there, strong and natural in the water, perhaps a onetime Channel swimmer, friendly to the lake despite its treachery, even though the situation is bleak. But he decides, finally, to make his way back to the ramp, a smooth, nondisruptive breaststroke that carries him slowly back to the woman. She is standing, leaning forward, her large, farm-wife hands pressed against her face. *Where are my babies?* leaks between the big-knuckled fingers, the mouth turning down, a burnt-umber crescent, the wide eyes—twin slashes of black with a #8 red sable brush. This, or: sinking to her knees, her long fingers tearing at her breasts, only now it is the black guitar, and the music she rakes out of it falls on the swimmer like shrapnel.

"Why are you crying, Smitty?" Miss Klein asks. "What's wrong?"

I let the darling chippy come to me. No more painting for today. "It's fucked," I say. She touches my face.

"*Why?*" she asks. Her tone is what her Social Welfare professors call "supportive." She means well, but she doesn't know what she means. She allows her virgin tits to nudge my trembling lips. She regards the blown painting. She whistles some breath between her perfect little teeth. "Oh, wow, Smitty," she says, sagging into me, her nipples erect with awe.

Dear Boss:

Forgive this intrusion, but we should have invented a ritual— I know, I know, you tried, with those white-gloved honor guards with their Napoleon hats and silver buckles, but I'm thinking of something more useful, something flashy but more democratic, something available to the great unwashed. Something to let them atone for this tendency of flesh and bone to dream itself rich. Unamerican, unamerican I hear you murmuring, but didn't we learn anything at all from our Big-Little Jungle War? Over there they kneel before stone idols and expect nothing back, not a dime. They take a swim in Exxon Hi-Test and then they light a match. We try to rev up desire, they try to extinguish it. We need a routine, something that will let us rev down. Sometimes, Boss, a step or two backwards is a great leap forward. But don't tell Neil I said that, he might not send me his hand. You thought I was such an ironic bastard. You would grin in your tightassed way, purse your lips, then tap your temple with one dancing finger, indicating the madness of things in general. Oh, Boss, you had perfect cynicism. No world leader could match it. The French were boy scouts compared to you. You even dismayed the jaded Russians. You had several extemporaneous gestures that indicated to the Inner Circle alone your wise and deadly grasp of the General Human Catastrophe. I remember how you gave the finger to Rocky when he turned his back on you at the reception for poor old Ike. Boss, even Billy Graham gave up on you. You were really something. The country doesn't know it now and probably never will, but it needed you, it really did.

Faithful in Exile,

Ben

I once taught International Law with amiable self-confidence at a fine eastern university, but now I am a student of the hardened moment. I have a nice collection of photos in which little yellow women nod over a row of body bags in which their babes have been sealed. But even the superior Nikon can't stop movement. Even the superior Nikon softens the moment. There is always the suggestion of "the next gesture," for the women seem ready to follow the bags underground. Their forward lean is unstoppable regardless of shutter speed. What stops the lean lies hidden in my paints. Hopper found it in umber, in blue, even in dead-white gesso.

Government service, at the decision-making level, draws in manics like a powerful magnet. What better place to engage the engines of hyper brain activity, and what greater depths are there to disappear into once the engine fails and the magnet reverses its polarization?

They tell me I'm a fine painter. (They don't see my aim or how I've failed. They give me my lithium and pat my back.) My work was exhibited on visitors' day. My first canvas received praise and was bought by the mayor of a nearby town. It was a dispassionate, sunset-red rendition of napalm. Symbolism is nothing more than irreducible realism. Realism that can be reduced is the ultimate fantasy. I'm talking about representationalism. Someone here tried to argue that Wyeth was better in every way than Hopper. I set him straight. Wyeth, I said, doesn't smell the brink, doesn't know how close it is. Hopper stands on the edge of it, staring down into the abyss, about to lose his balance, but heroically does not. Think about Soutine. The poor bastard fell in, headfirst, painted his pictures in the vertigo of free-fall. I'd like to paint a rigid side of beef, too, like Soutine. The snapped ribs fluorescent purple, the bright yellow fat. The sweetly cologned butcher idly cleavering the rugged joints. The business of art is not beauty. The business of art is to butcher whatever coddles the mind.

"But isn't life hard enough as it is, Smitty?" the chaplain asks.

"It's *too* hard. But bad art is just a blindfold for the guy about to be shot."

He lit his pipe and sucked thoughtfully, like a fatuous dean. "You're quite a puzzle to us, Smitty," he said.

My Dear Soutine:

Chaim, my friend, this much is true: there are always two of us in this landscape, baffled by rivers of wind, blond roads, furrows that subtend unnatural farms, and the inevitable distortion, my dear ulcered Jew—brutal eclipse of the land, birds strangled by trees, one memory of a flaccid nude, her red hands pressed to the broken sex. They came so suddenly that she had no time to take the smile off her face, and it lingers there, even as she bleeds into her fingers as two dozen storm troopers pull up their pants. The mud they shoved into her face remains uncut by tears. We've been here before, haven't we? You're long dead, I'll be gone eventually, but we'll be here again, close approximations at least, the conditions whitewashed as usual, yet always in the air the *thing* is available, all we have to do is look and not blink. We are children again, Chaim, unable to comprehend the lofty green mind that lifts the sky out of its socket, blisters the night with stars, drowns us in remorse. We assume *we* are guilty, that original sin stands unbroken and vital, and that the path to forgiveness is grown over or patrolled by tigers.

Your Devoted
Benedict Smith

My name isn't Benedict or Smith, but I like the dual suggestion of righteous treason and anonymity. It's saucy.

Maybe the problem lies in the woman's neck. Too elegantly long? Where is the suggestion of "beauty recoiling from its own false promise"? Is that what I meant? I don't know. She *is* beautiful. They always are. But isn't beauty the cruel light that shines on our wreckage?

The warden, an educated man with an M.S.W. from Berkeley, permits wives here once a month. Our is a psychosexually hip era. And we feel better for it, don't we? The statisticians have declared us free, free at last.

Helen (her name is not Helen) sits on my cot, horrified by the monklike simplicity of my new life. She is lovely as ever, more so now that personal disaster has slapped the girlish chat out of her. Gone too is the self-satisfied elegance of the highly placed wife, a style she was prepared to carry into middle age. Now she is wearing her years in her eyes. A beautiful despair broods in the hollows of her cheeks. I love her. I want her.

"Here, Ben?" she says, looking at the four plain walls of my room. "Here?"

"Sure. Here. Where else? The rec room? The squash court?"

She submits. We love like drowning swimmers, each pulling the other down into a private, inconsolable depth. We end up beached, sucking air. "Poor Helen," I say, touching her hand.

"Poor Ben," she says, touching mine.

(Lying in the cool yoke of her body, half asleep, I glimpsed them, the twin babies. My heart quivered. She felt it, squeezed my hand hard.)

"You had no energy when you were in government, Ben," she says. She speaks softly, into my shoulder.

But now all I have is energy. Country club life seals it up, concentrates it. If she has a lover (and I'm sure she has, for the distance between us is more than the simple distance of calamity and lost hope), then he is a work-ravaged functionary, full of impressive belief, serious with self-esteem, always looking ahead and never at the thing itself blooming in his hand.

(I am swimming down to them, the pale babies. They are mo-

tionless in the gelid water, and I take them in my arms, hugging
the cold, unresponsive flesh. I float slowly toward the green light
of day, weeping against the lake. They are so beautifully formed,
beautiful beyond understanding or mercy, the opened eyes large
and punishing.)

"I still love you, Helen," I say. "More now than before."

I make coffee in my aluminum pot. We sit at my small table,
measuring the growing distance between our words.

"My life . . . things *are* going well for me," she says.

"I can see that."

"Still, I . . . I feel so . . . *abandoned,* Ben," she says, and the tears
spill out of her lovable eyes. "This is so hard for me."

"Mere words cannot express my profound sorrow," I say. Her
face turns quickly, as if sharply slapped.

I've decided to try several studies of the milieu. These will avoid a
direct look at the tragedy. The stones, for instance, that line the
shore next to the boat ramp. Are they washed in the light of the
milky sun, or is there a small incandescence burning at their cores?
What are the qualities that give them the grim permanence they
truly own? And the lake itself. Where is the swimmer, how far
from the ramp, and can his eyes be seen, or his expression? Water
neither black nor blue, water without gleam, water like the broad
flat back of a prehistoric nightmare. And what does the closed
house stand against? Sky? Its own careful shadow? Has it been
stripped of its history, like a Hopper bungalow? In the public park
a softball game continues despite the arrival of the ambulance. Has
the pitcher taken something off his sinker? The players are white
figures against impossible green. The ball has just been slapped to
deep center, and all the players are facing the brooding trees beyond
the outfield, arms down. Good. See it there, the dead thing in
centerfield that expands toward us brutally in Hooker's Green,
Raw Sienna, and Cobalt Blue? Then the stones: six feet of canvas,
left to right, covered with carefully pocked stones. Dark water
glistens in the cracks like a million eyes. The house: white under
the tall sky, sinking into the dead grass around it, an unstable
woman in the doorway revealing her breasts, hoping someone will

pass by, but no one ever will. Through a gable a black slot stares out at us between the white curtains.

I try to paint the woman from the point of view of a once-trusted public official. He stands behind her, reading aloud from a uselessly subjective, somewhat hysterical report for which he will be demoted, exiled, and eventually fired. "The asshole," said the Boss, "wrote a *poem* to a gold star mother in Kansas!"

My Dear Lady:

Something the size
Of a baby's eyes
Floats in a Saigon gutter.
Marrow, soft as butter,
Leaks from a skull.
Dear Lady, there is no lull
In the general slaughter.
Pray, now, for your daughter.

Something in the way her shoulders lump, as if the canvas had become alive, and my perspective goes haywire with terror. The lake is rising, mystic tide, vertical blue barrier, and the sky, what's left of it, is a thin crimson band at the top, like a femur lifted out of a freshly shattered thigh. I am painting with my fists, my face, my tongue, and the easel rocks.

"What's *wrong*, Smitty?" says Miss Klein.

I am a dog, before her, on my knees, growling, nose in her tight hair. My face is wet with paint and tears.

"It was your *wife*, wasn't it?" she says sagely.

"Get dressed," I say. "We're through today."

"She seemed so *cold*, Smitty. You'd think six months . . ."

But I push her down with my war-painted face and down goes the canvas too. We slide together on top of it. She fucks with wholesome good-hearted intentions, but I have nothing but fear and token lust. She kisses the salt from my unkind eyes.

The swimmer is in deep water, embracing the babies. I paint a single grappling hook leaning against a red fender. Behind the wheel of the ambulance sits the Boss, tapping his finger against his forehead, giggling to himself. He is dressed in medical white, always the actor, always one step ahead of the rest of us. The swimmer's powerful legs thrust against the water as he surges toward air. The eye of one baby seems to be looking through us, focusing on something several miles behind our heads. ("Sentimental," whispers the Boss as he slips the key into the ignition.)

Miss Klein *likes* older men, it turns out. Their winded lungings touch her heart. Could I fill her with babies? "Miss Klein," I say, brush poised. "Would you marry me?"

"I'd have to think about it, Smitty," she says. "You already *have* a wife."

The sequence of her logic is lovely. She'd be a strong wife. She might regulate these abstract fits and starts.

The Boss once said, "Smitty, there's something flagrantly un*real* about all this." The big slide to nowhere had begun. "Look what they're doing to me! And for *what*? It isn't happening, none of it. That's the answer."

"It's happening, Boss," I said. We were tooling down Pennsylvania Avenue in the four-ton Lincoln. I used the radio to call a friend in Rio. These toys would soon belong to other players.

"I *know* it's happening," he said, peevish. "But can you fucking *believe* it? That's what I'm saying here."

Dear Boss:
Reality is not a joke, false as it is. And surrealism is unnecessary and represents, simply, the failure of the imagination. Dalí, essentially, is a con artist.

Ben

Dear Ben:
You remember that old Donovan number, First there is a mountain, then there is no mountain, then there is? Well, I am into that glorious third stage of life and I say fuck you and your precious Hopper. You say he declares the primacy of space and throws time out the window. Well, I say, Why

not kick space out that same window? You want to fuck with the rules, well, then, *really* fuck with the rules. Personally, Wyeth is my man: fellow sage in the third stage. Listen up: I'm dabbling in oils these days myself. Black holes—my topic. Black canvas with a single black dot in the middle of it. Hot gimmick, huh? Keep your sense of humor, Bub. Don't take yourself so seriously. Nobody likes a middle-aged bore. Do trees, Ben! Do mountains, do cows and horses, do pretty girls with big tits and old men with big warts, do oceans and rivers, do waving fields of grain! It's here to *enjoy*, dummy! Do dancers, do walkers, do motels, hotels, duplexes. Do skylines, do bums, do airports. And do the long, well-traveled, bright-tarred highways and byways. Get lost in it, my friend. Give up the ghost. What I'm saying is, do what you see, Ben. And always know this: I loved it. I loved it all, peaks and valleys. You've got to love it, otherwise you will always find yourself standing in the shit.

> *Ciao, de bono et malo*
> (Forgive the lack of a proper
> signature. I put my name to
> no documents these days.)

The swimmer has reached the surface. The drowned babies are in his arms. The woman's mouth is a black shiver across the skin of the world. I'm sorry, this is what I see.

The swimmer is treading water in the middle of the lake. He is unwilling to swim back to the ramp and the kneeling woman. He can hear her heart beating, thudding through her bones, down into the wet logs of the ramp, and out into the darkening water.

The swimmer's face in gesso. Like a paper face glued to certain Oriental dolls. So tiny out there in the dim, vast lake. This is what I see.

The amused eye of the Boss is on me. I've lost all skill and patience. My jerking hand is ruled now by my quaking gut. I don't know what I'm doing, Boss. I guess I never really did. Miss Klein is staring adorably into a daydream of consequence.

The Boss winks lewdly, guns the big engine of the ambulance. He leans on the horn with both arms. "Get your ass in gear, Smitty!" he yells. "I don't have all day! Get on with it, hot-shot!"

I pick up the heavy, paint-charged brush. It fits my hand, crude and lovely as a weapon.

The Flowers of Boredom

He would gladly make the earth a shambles
and swallow the world in a yawn.
—Baudelaire, *Au Lecteur*

*L*amar sits in his office near the end of the day looking out at the bent heads of the sixteen men who work for him. The men appear to be engrossed in a new manual that reviews company policy concerning the cost-effectiveness of redundant systems intended to upgrade product reliability. The product is a vital part for a proposed new Mach 3 bomber that carries the informal in-house designation Big Buck. Big Buck will probably never be produced, or, if it is, it will most likely be awarded to a company headquartered in Texas, onetime home of the vice president. Favors, like hard currency, are always paid back in Washington. The deck is stacked, as usual, and Lamar's company, Locust Airframes, Inc., is close to the bottom of this one. Still, this going-through-the-motions is necessary, and profitable in itself since the Buyer—in this case the Air Force—picks up the tabs for these ritual dances the Defense Industry puts on. Lamar's sixteen men are part of the dance, recently hired to fatten the payroll roster of Advanced Proposals Engineering (APE), the section of Locust Airframes whose mission is to bid for contracts. Lamar himself is a new man insofar as he has been promoted from the rank of Reliability Engineer Step III to full-fledged Manager. This has involved a change of ID badge color from tepid aqua to radiant orange, an upgraded wardrobe, modifications in demeanor, and a tidy jump in salary and benefits. Job security, of course, is still tied to the shifting sands of Department of Defense wants and desires, which are always creatures of the latest Red Threat Scenario and not necessarily a realistic response to the international situation. Lamar has been around long enough to know better—thirteen years now—but he's impressed by his good fortune anyway. He now has his own secretary instead of having to share a pool typist. She is a new employee also, and has eyes for him already. Eyes, that is, for Management. Power, Lamar knows, is one of the more dependable aphrodisiacs. Lamar encourages a protective cynicism in himself, but he's only human and knows he would be stupid to look this splendid gift horse in the mouth.

The window in his office is one-way glass, allowing Lamar to observe his sixteen men while cloaked in smoky invisibility. The situation, Lamar muses, is analogous to that of a god looking down from a screen of clouds at the unhappy mortals below who believe with touching urgency that their frenetic schemes and counter-schemes are extensions of conscious ideals. The god maintains this illusion in order to hold the level of human unhappiness constant. He ensures that the noblest projects of those he rules become the *means* of their unhappiness. *Lamar, Lamar*, Lamar thinks, chiding himself for such bloated fantasies. *Where do you get such ideas?* He has a partial memory of where such ideas came from—a walk in the dark with a fallen angel—but no, that's literature, something he read years ago in college. In any case, the fantasy is benign, since Lamar has genuine sympathy for his men. He knows, for instance, that he is also being monitored by Middle Management— carefully jealous men who are halfway up the corporate ladder and do not intend to be bumped by an ambitious underling who doesn't know the rules of climbing. *We are all in the same boat, friends*, Lamar thinks as he looks out at the round-shouldered men. *It's just that I'm on a higher deck than you.*

Lamar sees that one of his new men is hiding his near-baldness with wings of yellowish-white hair stretched over his dome from the thriving area above his right ear. The man is in his fifties and is lucky to have been hired at all. This is likely to be the last job he will ever have in the Defense Industry. After the contract has been let to the Texas company the ax will fall and the sixteen men, along with Lamar himself, will be sent scrambling for other positions within the company. The bald man in his fifties will be cut loose. Age isn't his only albatross. His relatively high salary makes his tenure an impossibility during the austere period that follows a lost contract. And his chances outside the Defense Industry are nil. Companies that are connected to legitimate free-enterprise adventures, such as IBM, AT&T, or the small but highly efficient consulting firms, want no part of men who have spent their adult lives in the Defense Industry. Men such as Lamar's bald man are not what the want ads refer to as "self-starters." Their ponderous, insouciant demeanor makes the personnel interviewers shake their heads in smiling dismay.

The bald man, Lamar knows, has been in the Defense Industry since the 1950s. B.S. in electrical engineering from Fresno or San Jose State, but has by now forgotten most of his elementary calculus and differential equations. He is what is known in the business as a "Warm Body." The Air Force, before letting a contract, likes to see a company have enough self-confidence to maintain a large, well-paid work force. This results in extreme overhiring in the months before a big contract is about to come down. Lamar has been raised to Management to preside over sixteen Warm Bodies. He doesn't mind—it's the system. But only the middle-aged bald man *knows* he is a Warm Body. The others are naïve kids, a few years out of college, though the more intelligent ones are becoming restless. They glance, blindly, from time to time at the smoked glass of Lamar's office as if to ask, "Isn't there anything for me to *do*?" Sometimes the blind glance is sharply suspicious—premature inklings of what the bald man knows.

The bald man cannot do real work, anyway. No one expects him to. He, and others like him, have made their homes through the decades of cold war in places such as Boeing, Lockheed, North American, or McDonnell Douglas, where they grew dim and paunchy reading turgid manuals while dreaming of overseas travel, golf, or a resurrected sexual urge. If such a man is approaching old age and has given up on the vigorous pastimes, it's possible that the simplest pleasures, such as good strong bowel movements or freedom from stiff joints, occupy his reverie. He is terrorized now and again by the streaky pains in his pectorals and arm, sudden sieges of caffeine-instigated vertigo, or shortness of breath. He is probably well past caring about his wife's slow evolution toward complete and self-sufficient indifference. Lamar is not without compassion for the bald man, who was born without ambition, yet who once had all the appetites ambition serves. Now he just wants to stay comfortably alive.

Lamar is sympathetic because he knows that he is not substantially different from the bald man. They are brothers in the same tribe. Lamar's single advantage, he believes, is that he knew—and *liked*—the rules of the game when he first hired in, thirteen years ago. He seems to have been born with an instinctive grasp of what the system likes to see in a new man. Early in his career he learned how to appear innovative and energetic while at the same time assuring his superiors that these alarming qualities were empty of substance. And though he was ambitious, he understood the politics of ambition: Never frighten the man immediately above you on the ladder. He is in an excellent position to stomp on your head.

It's a Byzantine institution, the Defense Industry, with its own rules, rituals, and arcana that confuse and frustrate the uninitiated. And yet it manages to produce weapons of ever-increasing sophistication. That some of these weapons do not work is beside the point, a quibble rooted in a fundamental misunderstanding of the mission of the Defense Industry, which is, simply, to keep itself well nourished with Cost-Plus money, to increase steadily in manpower and physical plant, and to reveal itself to the gullible citizenry as an economic savior as well as a vital necessity in a dangerous world. In any case, most of the weapons *do* work, eventually, if not after the first production run of operational units. As long as the fabulous deep pocket of Cost-Plus money is reachable, the missiles will find their targets, the bombers will get off the ground, and the submarines will float. Lamar's Reliability Section is the arm of Locust Airframes that devotes itself to the creation of documents that further this notion. Reliability achieved through redundant components is costly, but as the number of additional backup systems increases on a given piece of equipment, the theoretical failure-rate dwindles steadily toward the infinitesimal. It's as if men were equipped with one or two extra hearts, or had fresh, supple arteries ready to back up their old, cholesterol-choked ones should they fail. Reliability is the dream of immortality transferred to electronics, hydraulics, and structural mechanics.

With nothing much to do himself, Lamar now studies the stiffening necks of the younger men in his section. They are primed for significant action. They are bright, hardworking, and very well trained. The system will blunt their keen appetites for real work and discourage their desire to understand their jobs better by gaining an overview of the entire operation of Locust Airframes, from design to production. Only a chosen few have such indispensable omniscience. And these few are never seen by men such as Lamar's. Soon, the better of these young engineers will become deeply frustrated and resign. Though Lamar is not old—not quite forty—the sight of the young engineers makes him feel a fatigue rightfully belonging to a man twenty years older. It's their clear-eyed visionary look; the look that tells you they believe in what they are doing and that it makes a real difference to the geopolitical future of the planet. They haven't understood yet that boredom is the soil in which they must grow, if they are to stay on. The soil of boredom is gray, which is the color of the walls, the desks, and the carpeting. Lamar has thrived in this gray soil, a hardy survivor, like mesquite or wild rose. These moments of spiritual fatigue are few. And though he prefers to wear gray suits, his neckties are always bold. The effect is: Ambition Under Control.

Across the street from Advanced Proposals Engineering is a topless bar called The Web. Lamar comes here every day after work for a pick-me-up. The Web owes its existence to APE, its clientele consisting of engineers, secretaries, and the occasional Manager. And spies. Lamar remembers a time here when two thickset men in three-piece suits handcuffed and searched a man wearing an engineer's badge. "Spy," the bartender told him. "The Feds have had their eyes on him for months. The guy drank nothing but lime rickeys like it was summer in Havana. You can spot the type a mile off."

Lamar was required to watch a film, when he first was hired by Locust, that warned about spies. "The pleasant chap occupying the desk next to yours might be an agent of the Communist conspiracy." The narrator was Ronald Reagan—a young, pre-officeholding Ronald Reagan—and the tone of the film was McCarthy-era serious. The statistics given were certified by the FBI. "There may be as many as four hundred spies operating in your plant. Think about it." Lamar thought about it but never saw much in the way of suspicious activity. He never saw much in the way of *any* kind of activity, except in the factory areas themselves. But in the vast office buildings all he saw was the interminable browsing through documents by men fighting a grass-roots existential conviction that a cancer of meaninglessness had taken root in their lives.

Once a pleasant man from Hungary, a refugee, was hauled out of the desk next to Lamar's by armed guards. It turned out the man had not been totally candid about his political affiliations when he hired into Locust. He'd been a member of the Communist Party in Hungary, before the 1956 revolt, though he'd renounced it shortly afterward. But he left this chapter of his life off his personnel data sheet. The man had a name the other engineers joked about— Dumb-a-link Banjo Wits, something like that. Dumbalink was a fierce and outspoken anti-Communist and American patriot, but was taken away in handcuffs and never heard from again. Lamar had liked Dumbalink Banjo Wits and had called Security with the intention of telling them that the Hungarian made most of the engineers in his section look like fellow travelers by comparison, but Security wasn't interested. "He fibbed," the bored Security man had told Lamar.

Lamar, lost in bourbon daydreams, hasn't noticed that someone has slipped into the booth and is sitting opposite him. It's his secretary, a tall, olive-skinned girl with hair so blond it hurts his eyes when he finally looks up. Her name is Theresa Keyser but she has told him to please call her "Terry." Lamar has fixed her age at twenty-nine, though her job application said twenty-five.

"So, this is where you disappear to," Terry says, smiling. Her blue eyes are intense and, it seems to Lamar, too confident.

"My second home," Lamar says, lifting his bourbon and winking.

"Meanwhile, dinner is in the oven in your *first* home."

Lamar is annoyed, but her smile is splendidly straightforward. It makes him believe that she is being aggressive out of nervousness. "Hell," he says, "*APE* is my first home," and she laughs the tension out of her voice and touches his hand.

"I'll have a gimlet," she says to him, though the barmaid, a topless girl with spiders tattooed on her breasts, has been waiting to take her order.

They have two drinks apiece, their conversation gradually changing from office talk to the more revealing narratives alcohol inspires. Lamar learns that Terry has been married and divorced twice and is now unattached. He doesn't try to characterize his own decade-long marriage beyond suggesting that his wife's interests and his own have diverged somewhat over the years. He tells her this in a joking, cavalier manner: his views of marriage are a mixture of fatalism and the always optimistic belief in renewable relationships. This is California, after all, the land of expected transformations. Terry laughs easily at his bittersweet jokes—maybe too easily—but Lamar appreciates it anyway. He likes her, sees that she is intelligent and that her expectations are sober and under control. He reaches across the table and touches her hand. She takes his wrist and applies brief but significant pressure. Her eyes, which had been bold, are now disturbingly vulnerable. *Jesus,* Lamar thinks, knowing that three bourbons and water have inflamed some old romantic notions, *here we go.*

The barmaid brings them two more drinks. "Compliments of the sport in the rubber sandals," she says, gesturing toward a man in a black suit seated at the bar. The man is watching TV—a game show—and is wearing white socks and lipstick-red sandals. He is a Howard Hughes look-alike, trying to create the impression of "renegade genius gone seedy." Even his stringy hair is long and unwashed. The man, sensing Lamar's peevish gaze, looks at him and waves his swizzle stick. His smile is a yellow leer. Lamar knows something about that leer, has seen it before, and is about to tell the barmaid to take the drinks away when Terry returns the man's swizzle-stick salute and says, "Thanks!" just like that, loud enough to make several heads turn toward their booth.

And then it hits Lamar that he knows the man in the rubber sandals. He was a high-level Procurement Manager for Locust a few years ago. Lamar, in fact, had worked for him when he first hired into Locust. Then there was a big cutback and the man was caught in the middle of an in-company war of attrition. He lost out to men who were more adroit in making the company classify them as indispensable. "Voss," Lamar says, under his breath. When Terry looks at him with raised eyebrows, he says, "Randy Voss. Used to be a wheel. He was supposed to be in line for company president. Crazy genius, they used to say. He must have jumped when he should have ducked."

Lamar is a little rocky when they finally leave The Web. On their way out the door they have to pass by Randy Voss. "Departing so soon?" Voss says to them. Up close his yellow leer is a toxic stain. "The evening is still young, kids. Tell you what, let's make a killer night of it. I'm still fat." He takes out his wallet and taps the bar with it.

Terry starts to answer but Lamar takes her arm and pulls her along. What she doesn't know is that the old ex-Manager is a degenerate who thinks it would be nice if the three of them could get together in a downtown motel, in the wino district, and play out some rank fantasy starring himself. Lamar has heard all the Randy Voss stories. When the man had power the stories had the glitter of outré high times. Now he's just flea meat; another unremarkable scumbag.

It's almost dark outside. Terry takes Lamar's arm as they cross the street to the Locust parking lot. "Are you going to come over?" she asks, leaning toward him.

Lamar looks at his watch. "It's late," he says.

"Do you care?"

She lives in a fourplex, upstairs, the view of the ocean blocked by a new high-rise condo that has been painted the slate-gray color of the ocean under a winter overcast. "They know how to break your heart, don't they?" Lamar says, mostly to himself.

Terry makes Lamar a bourbon and water and a gimlet for herself. Lamar carries his drink in the palm of his hand as he tours the small apartment. "You do this?" he asks, nodding at a murky painting of a western scene.

"I'm afraid so," she says modestly. "I take art in night school."

"Nice."

"Do you like the condor?"

Lamar leans toward the painting, which is hanging over the sofa. A bird—it looks like a crow to him—is suspended in midair above a lumpish road-kill on a desert highway.

"It's about to feast on that overripe deer," she explains.

Crow or condor, the bird seems incapable of flight. A stone bird with cast-iron wings. The deer is generic meat, a formless wedge of brown paint streaked with crimson.

"I call it *The Angel of Death*," Terry says. "But maybe that's too trite. I think I'll change it to *Feast of Life*. I don't know. I'm torn. What do you think?"

She is standing close to him. He can see her lungs move as she breathes, the rise and fall of her sweater. He begins to see her details: the small, nearly black mole just above her collarbone, the finely scented neck hair, the lovely cut of her lips and nostrils. He slips his arm around her and she looks up at him, lips parting for the kiss. He kisses her chilly lips, and then they both put down their drinks and kiss again, with heat.

"I vote for *Feast*," he says. "*Feast of Life*."

Lamar wakes from a dream frightened, unable to tell himself where he is. He is reasonably sure he is not home. The rumble of traffic outside is not familiar. His heart is beating light and fast, like an engine in too high a gear to have any power. His fear begins to escalate into panic. It's happened to him before. He has a method for calming himself down. He begins with his name, the color of his hair and eyes, the ghost-white scar on his left forearm. He makes a list of keystone events: the year he was born, the years he graduated high school and college, the year he got married, and the name of the town he and his wife had eloped to. In this way he gradually finds himself. He reaches over and touches the woman next to him. She makes a sound he does not recognize as she turns over to face him.

"Theresa Keyser," he says, not *addressing* but naming her.

"Are you still here?" she says, picking up her clock radio to study its dial. "Shouldn't you get home?"

His memory, set in motion by the emergency Lamar has declared, continues to fill him in: an image of the man he had forgotten about, the degenerate ex-Manager, Randy Voss, comes to him unbidden. Voss is saying something to him. They are walking, ten or more years ago, near an Assembly-and-Checkout Area of the plant. Missiles on huge transport vehicles are slipping slowly out of a black building. It is a rainy night. Voss is laughing—*crazily*, Lamar thinks. "Nobody knows Jack shit," Voss is saying to Lamar. "If you are going to stay in this business, you've got to remember that. Something else, something besides men and machines gets all this fancy work done."

Lamar, watching the glistening missiles slide through the rain, thinks he understands what Voss is telling him. A missile, a bomber, a sub—they are all jigsaw puzzles, the pieces made all over the country. The men who make the individual pieces don't know— or need to know—the purpose of their work. The pieces are assembled by other bored functionaries who are also ignorant of the big picture.

"I see what you mean," Lamar says.

"No you don't. You really don't," Voss says. "What I am telling you is that there is a great dark . . . *consensus* . . . that sweeps things along to their inevitable conclusion. There is an intelligence behind it, but, believe me, it is not human. It is the intelligence of *soil*, the thing that lifts trees and flowers out of the ground. I am too astonished and thrilled to be frightened by it."

Lamar saw, even then, that Randy Voss was crazy, but what he had said made a lasting impression. And over the years he has come to adopt Voss's idea as his own. But it was something he was unable to talk about to anyone else, not even his wife. How could you convince anyone that in this industry no single individual, or group of individuals, suspects the existence of a vital sub rosa mechanism that produces and deploys our beautifully elegant weapons? How could you *say* to someone that the process is holistic, that a headstrong organic magic is at work, or that a god presides?

Pagans

The gray Bavarian yodeling in the bathroom sent the New Year's party into a terminal slump. It was Dr. Selbiades's annual get-together for his patients. I'd been there less than an hour and had watched the party go from white-knuckle cheerfulness to unapologetic gloom.

Selbiades had been my shrink for almost a year. He was known as Doc Dow, after the chemical company. He believed in psychoactive drugs, not psychology. Psychology, he said, is rooted in semantics and semantics is rooted in the mind and the mind is a myth. There is the brain, the central nervous system, and there is the World. Sometimes they don't mesh. Chemistry is learning how to make them mesh. "We're in the Model T era of psychopharmacology," he once said. "The future is gleaming with Volvos, BMWs, and Ferraris."

I believed him. Why shouldn't I have? The yodeling Bavarian only last year was a cataleptic wallflower in the State Hospital. One dose of a new compound and he was goose-stepping to Wagner and asking for beefy women. I'd been brought from severe, broad-spectrum anxiety to chronic sulkiness in less than a year. I expected, any day now, a new ordering of the psychoactive rainbow to nudge me into a semipersistent state of kindhearted tolerance. Nirvana, according to Doc Dow, always happens on the molecular level, regardless of the method used to achieve it. Without drugs it takes Spartan restrictions of sensory inputs, dietary extremism, and a kind of self-hypnosis. Our Puritanical heritage, said the Doctor, makes us scoff at the notion that spiritual bliss can be gotten by swallowing capsules. But we are learning how to play the brain note by note, he said.

I was still a half-turn out of tune. It made me snappish and fussy. I affronted strangers for reasons I could not later explain. The yodeling Bavarian in the Selbiadeses' shower was a good example. He had wanted the tiled walls of the shower to call up the effect of sheer alpine slopes so that he could show us how it had been with him when he was a Nazi ski trooper during the War. I was in the bathroom at the time, taking my second Elavil of the evening. The Bavarian had left the bathroom door open so that everyone could hear him. When I went out, I closed the door behind me. His yodels softened to a chirping lament. The stiffly seated guests looked at me, some with anger in their eyes, some with cruel hilarity. All rode the black horse Despair.

"Some Nazi bastard like him killed my uncle," I said to the group. It was a lie, but I was shameless. That was another feature of my untuned brain. Cheap lies. I used them like salt and pepper. They gave an edge to the watery soup of my life.

I put on my parka and cap. "Leaving us so soon?" said Beth Selbiades, the Doctor's stunning wife. What a full-blown, fine-haired animal you are, I wanted to say, but one does not speak churlishly to the high priest's wife.

"Got to get home," I finally mumbled.

I went out into a whirlwind of snowflakes. A warm, southerly blizzard had moved in, blanketing our town with heavy wet snow, pretty to remember from the safety of July, but a misery to stroll through. I was dressed for it, except for my shoes, which were loafers.

I had walked out of my own New Year's party. Raquel had kissed Sloan Capoletti, our milkman, hours before midnight. I took umbrage. Having been out of work for some time, I was oversensitive to the carefree revels of the employed. Sloan had been giving us free cottage cheese (unsalable cheese that had survived its expiration date) because he felt sorry for our economic plight. Or so I thought. Then, as I watched the prolonged, open-mouth kiss, I understood that his dated cheese was meant to woo. After the hot kiss under that parasitic tree-killer, mistletoe, they went into the kitchen where Sloan showed Raquel how to brew saloop, a hot drink made of sassafras, sugar, and milk. A blood purifier, Sloan said. I was suspicious. Why did Raquel keep sassafras in her spice and herb cupboard? To please the milkman? Excellent for the bowels, Sloan said. Why did the milkman want the bowels of my wife to be excellent? The party became a forest of symbols, all of them unfriendly to me, even dangerous—pagan symbols, witch symbols: mistletoe, sassafras, and scented candles, the over-decorated Christmas tree fat and gaudy as an old whore leaning drunkenly in the corner. And then, as if I'd been the victim of an openly wicked practical joke, I began to receive heartening winks from total strangers. I needed to walk.

I put on my parka and watch cap. Raquel cornered me in the hallway. "What do you think you're doing?" she said.

I gave her the look I felt she deserved. "He's in love with you," I said.

"I know," she said.

"You *know*?" I felt dizzy as my blood pressure wobbled and peaked.

"Of *course* I know!" she said, with unashamed spunk. "It's very harmless. He's a cute guy, Sloan is."

All I could do was stare at her as I zipped up the parka.

"Love is not harmless," I said, measuring out the words with some care.

She slapped her forehead and rolled her eyes. "Jesus, *listen* to what you are saying for once," she said. She turned away from me and walked back into the chaos of tooting horns, paper streamers, and the wet mouths of strangers. It was midnight in the eastern time zone, two hours away, but that was reason enough to toot your horn and stick your tongue down someone's throat.

I slammed the door behind me and started walking the seven blocks to Dr. Selbiades's house. The planet had French-kissed itself through several time zones as it mindlessly rolled down its doomed orbit. Though bells were ringing, horns were tooting, champagne corks were popping, I skulked away from it all, hating the manic pagans and their endless whoopee.

After I left the Selbiadeses' party, I walked aimlessly. I wandered into the North Side, a poorly lit district of tall Victorian houses. The area was famous for night crimes. Muggings, rapes, vandalism were the nocturnes played in these shadowy streets and alleys. I half expected a mugger to put a knife to my throat, and didn't care. Then a man waved to me from a front porch. He was a tall, heavy man in a metallic green suit. "That you, Roger?" he asked.

I shrugged. "Why not?" I answered.

"Then come on in, we've been waiting to start. Did you get lost or something?"

"Yes and no," I said.

I climbed the sagging boards of the porch stairs. When I reached the big man, he threw his arms around me. "Peg Munson is nervous as hell," he whispered into my ear, his warm spittle electrifying it. "I'm Jerry Peters," he said, pumping my hand. "You know," he added, seeing my blank look, "group coordinator."

He took my arm and steered me into the house. Inside, seated on sofas, love seats, and armchairs, were about a dozen people, men and women in their late thirties or early forties. "Here's the missing person," Jerry said, slapping me on the back. "Roger"— he fumbled with a piece of paper, a computer printout, squinted at it—"Roger *Flexnor*. Now we can get the show on the road."

It was easy to figure out that everyone here was a stranger to everyone else and that Roger Flexnor, whoever he was, was expected to round out the group: six males, six females. I guessed it was some kind of dating club for hopeless cases. I felt right at home.

People on one of the sofas scooted over, making room for me. I sat between a pale, bearded man and a small, plump woman. "I'm Peg Munson," the woman said.

I shook her hand. "Roger Flexnor," I said.

"Where's your data sheet?" she said.

I slapped my coat pockets, dug in my pants.

"Here's an extra," Peg Munson said, giving me a carefully folded computer printout. I saw her name, a paragraph giving a general (somewhat generous) physical description, and a personal statement ("Professional woman, Master's degree, likes walks in the rain, poetry that speaks directly to the soul, good conversation over gourmet dinners; expects to share her considerable resources, both physical and spiritual, with a man of corresponding substance").

I refolded the data sheet and slipped it into my pocket, wondering what Roger Flexnor had to offer such a woman.

". . . tall, scientifically oriented man," Peg read, from the data sheet of Roger Flexnor, "desires *affaire d'amour* with mature Christian lady with unusually small features . . ." She giggled self-consciously; then, splaying her fingers in her lap, revealed to me a set of miniature hands without visible knuckle. This is what Roger Flexnor desired most in a woman. I glanced down at her feet and saw that they were also miniatures. Flexnor would be seriously awash in lust by now.

Jerry Peters, our host, said, "All right, one and all, let's get right down to it. We're not children, and it's a brand-new year. At least it will be in fifteen minutes. There's no need to stumble and bumble. I suggest we break with the past, whatever *that* might be, and give our Rocky Mountain Dating Service partners a big how-do-you-do Happy New Year kiss."

A woman, almost as big as Jerry Peters, stood up and kissed him with shocking energy. I leaned toward Peg Munson and she closed her eyes and offered me her Kewpie-doll lips.

"You're shy," she said, after the pecking kiss. "I am too. I guess the computer knows how to match personality types."

Peg Munson not only had little hands and feet, she also had tiny facial features. Lips, nose, and eyes were set close to one another to produce a smallish face. Her head was a distraction: it was nearly full-sized. "I've always wanted to know a Christian man who had a passion for nuclear science," she said, breathy with growing interest.

Then the real Roger Flexnor came in. "Sorry, everybody," he said, stamping snow off his shin-high mukluks. "I just could *not* get the chains on my car. I had to have the Exxon people do it." He was a tall, white-haired man in heavy glasses.

"Who are *you?*" Jerry Peters said.

"I'm Roger. Roger Flexnor, Ph.D. You're expecting me. I'm here for Peg Munson." He waved his printout as his glasses fogged over in the warm room.

I got up and walked through the awkward silence until I was back out on the street. The street seemed the place for me that New Year's Eve.

Jerry Peters called to me from the porch. "Hey, it's okay, citizen," he said. "Next time, though, try going through Central Data. We've got uplinks throughout the Northwest. Check out our ad in tomorrow's paper. There's someone out there who loves you. Believe it."

I didn't believe it. I waved to him and walked toward downtown, another two or three miles into the wind.

The city streets were bright with holiday decorations, but empty. I went into the first bar I came to, a place I'd never been in, called The Loose Caboose, a velveteen-and-Leatherette night spot with a scandalous reputation, but I was cold, and brave with self-pity.

The Loose Caboose was nearly empty. One drunk in a three-piece suit at the bar, two guys in designer sweats huddled in a booth. A big TV over the bar was showing us what New Year's Eve in New York was like. I ordered a bourbon and soda, and then another. An oily, old-time band singer in a tux began his version of "I'll Take Manhattan," Times Square celebrants roaring behind him.

My feet were aching with cold. The third bourbon made them feel like they were Roger Flexnor's feet.

"I know utter dejection when I see it," said one of the designer sweat-suit guys. He was at the bar, ordering drinks for himself and his friend, but looking at me.

"Good for you," I said.

"Say, listen," he said. "Delvin and I are going dancing later. You want to tag along? My name is Jeffrey, Jeffrey Hazeltine."

Delvin came up behind me. He put his arm around my shoulders. "Do I get the first dance or not?" he said to me, his voice sharp with a habitual pout.

"Not," I said.

Outside The Loose Caboose I realized that the walk back home was close to four miles and most of it was uphill. I jerked the strings of my parka hood tight and set out.

Three blocks into my trek, a car pulled alongside me. It was the pair from The Loose Caboose. "You need a ride?" Delvin asked.

"I need a ride *home*," I said.

"Hop in."

I did. I sat in the back while the two friends cuddled up front. I held no opinions about all this. Opinion holding had been one of the first casualties of my condition. Not that I didn't have opinions, I just didn't *hold* them. Everything was open to dispute, mutation, or outright cancellation.

I had an opinion about everything that had happened to me that evening, but also knew that I would not defend it tomorrow even if I could remember what it was. It seemed to me that all the people I had been with were puppets to a hidden agony, and could not find simple peace until the puppet master had lost interest in them. They had been yanked down their lives with seismic disregard. They didn't know where they were. They wanted their bearings and were willing to risk a lot to find them.

I revised this opinion a few times before giving it up. I wished the whole stumbling lot of us a lucky New Year. Then I remembered Sloan Capoletti. I leaned into the front seat. "Drive faster, Jeffrey," I said.

Mole

We believe they are escalating their operations. You know who I mean. I cannot name names. They get at you. Therefore I carry the gun wherever I go. Orders. Regulations. Procedures. It isn't much of a weapon but it can do the job. It is better than nothing. A snub-nosed .32 lightweight. A belly gun. You've seen them. It fits my hand so well only the short barrel can be seen. I've painted it fleshtone so that if I raise it in public they will think I am merely pointing. Look, I imagine them saying. The man with the swollen fist is pointing at something he finds interesting. He must be a tourist in our wonderful city. I assure you I am not now nor have I ever been a tourist in this or any other wonderful city.

It doesn't bother me. If they talk about me in this way. In fact, I feel successful when they do. Covered. His stupid coat is so bulky, I imagine them saying. That is the flak jacket under it. Which they do not see. I wear it at all times. In case of surprise attack. Orders. Regulations. Procedures. I can show you chapter and verse, paragraph and sentence. Et cetera. Gun, flak jacket, coding device. And, of course, the implanted communications center. Subdermal, gluteal, cranial. Which functions in the postmicrowave range to avoid intercepts. "We must be prepared for the Reckoning." (Control.)

You may think I am perfect. I'm sorry, you are wrong. I made a serious tactical mistake last evening. It happens. I hesitate to record it. Control is stern. Discipline day and night, and yet there are lapses. I went out to get Elaine's prescription filled. Her zombie pills. That's what I call them privately. Foolishly, she had let herself run out of them. I rarely go out past ten but she bawled and yanked her hair. So I went.

The streets of this city are not safe at night. They are out there. You know who I mean. I had walked three blocks before I realized my error. I forgot my gun. Will you believe it? I forgot my gun. I reached back under my coat to check my wallet and discovered the absent bulge. Instantly my knees unlocked. The streetlights danced. I went down. Bang against a mail drop, down on my side, over into the gutter. The breaker-breaker in my head did not rouse me. I dreamed briefly. Long-dead legs opening as we float on the leaves of strange melody. The flak jacket protected my ribs. Perhaps it only lasted one second. Or two. The grouped Negroes looked at me. I looked back. We looked at each other. I will not be looked at with impunity. I got up and dusted myself. Slowly. Carefully. In no hurry to get down the street. Irregular beats gripped my heart. Yet I smiled.

I walked the remaining fourteen blocks to Walgreen's. The pharmacist said, "You all right, Jim?" My name is of course not Jim or anything like Jim. His false familiarity was meant to demean. And yet I didn't take offense. It compliments my cover if they think me the fool.

I handed him the prescription. "Nearly expired," he said.

"Get the pills," I said.

"Stay cool, James Bond," he said, then went to his back room.

His remark stopped me. Perhaps he was one of them. You know who I mean. Do not think that only intellectual white men are traitors.

It took him twenty minutes to make up the capsules. Ten minutes too long. I tasted bile. The floor rose and fell. Rose and fell. Rose. Fell. I tried to remember: Where had I left my little pink gun? In my weaving mind I retraced my steps for the past several hours. I could not remember them all.

"Here you go, James," he said, sliding the bottle of pills toward me.

"I'm sick," I said.

"I'll get you something," he said.

I looked at him hard. What would he get me? Sodium pentothal? Cyanide? Microchip implant? "No," I said. "Nothing. I'm fine."

"You look green," he said. "You want Maalox?"

"Dramamine," I said. "Some Dramamine."

He got them. I paid. He watched me as I took several tablets without water. "Learn to make do." (Control.)

I walked home slowly. A casual saunter past the loitering races. "A fearless man with an easy mind," I imagined them saying, in their argot of choice. It wasn't easy. I felt naked without my gun. I wanted badly to trot. But Control says, A running agent stands out like a belly dancer in church. He violates the social tempo. When undercover heed the social tempo. It wasn't easy. Every passing car had a possible hunter-hawk agent in it. His Uzi rising to the window, aimed at my knees. Passersby disguised as dowager-humped Italian crones carried poison-tipped umbrellas ready to peck at my legs. They get at you. You know who I mean.

A skeleton in an iron-gray bathrobe popped out of a doorway directly in front of me. I fought successfully the impulse to drop to all fours and roll. The head gleamed. As if lacquered. The head had large empty eye sockets. The vast grin exposing long brown teeth. The twin nose holes big as quarters. A skull. "Dominique!" it screamed into my face. I prayed for my heart. Do not my Lord let it stop. Save me. That the light of day will once again touch my face. Help. "Dominique!" he crowed. A thin cat ran between his legs. He nodded to me. An old man, fleshless. "My kitty," he said. "Dominique." He backed slowly into his apartment. Still smiling.

I looked around to see if anyone had witnessed the encounter. There was no one in the street. A condition not to be taken at face value. I stared into each closed door. Each blind window. The rooftops. I fought back a delayed gag reflex. The skeleton who had called his kitty reeked. The breath fecal. The wind of decayed meat blown in my face.

How long had I been out? One hour? Two? A wrongness in the air struck me as I entered my apartment. I leaned in the jamb, confused. The notion that I had been tricked out of the house occurred to me. I recalled the delaying tactics of the pharmacist. His pointless conversation. My attack of dizziness. And why Walgreen's? Why not the Rexall, eight blocks closer?

Everything seemed normal enough. But it was in the air. Subtle change. I listened. I expected a communication from Control. The airwaves were dead. I could hear the TV. I knew the program. Small-arms warfare in a Third World jungle. Then two throats cleared themselves. I went in. Elaine was where I had left her. On the sofa. I rattled the bag from Walgreen's. A man in dungarees sat next to her. There was a drink in his hand. He had red hair and a fat red nose. His shoes were off. Though he had the appearance of a workman, he had the demeanor of a guest. I am trained to notice these subtle differences.

"Did you get them?" Elaine asked.

"Yes."

"What took you so long? Don't you realize I am ill? I woke up Mr. Lewis. I was frightened. There were snakes in the carpet. You know how I get."

"I went to Walgreen's."

"Why so far? Why not Rexall's?"

Mr. Lewis yawned but did not trouble to cover his large mouth, which, I noticed, was stained red.

"You said Walgreen's," I said.

"I said drugstore. Just drugstore. Give them to me."

I handed her the capsules. She went into the bathroom to take some. "She pounded the hell out of my door," Mr. Lewis said. "She looked terrible. So I came over to sit with her while you were out. Fella, you should never let Elaine run out of those pills."

Elaine. I decided to test him, then and there. "Our fine vintage is best," I said carefully. Code.

He held up his glass, looked at the liquid. "Not bad," he said, failing. I smiled inwardly. Then outwardly. If he was not one of ours, was he one of theirs? You know who I mean.

Elaine came in, also smiling. The zombie-pill smile. Loose, the eyelids drooping. Her feet slapping the floor recklessly. "Quit fighting, you two," she said.

"I'd better shove off," Mr. Lewis said.

"I won't hear of it," Elaine said, taking his arm and dragging him down to the couch. I sat beside them. "The movie is only half over. We were enjoying it. Weren't we, Bill?" Zombie hostess. Zombie charm.

"These guys," said Mr. Lewis, "play hardball. They go after Red spics."

"Do tell," I said, bored with Hollywood pablum.

The couch sagged. Elaine and Mr. Lewis are heavy. I am not. My end was up, theirs was down. They leaned into each other as the couch sagged further. Remembering the gun, I got up and went to the bedroom. It was not on the dresser. Or in with my socks. I went into the bathroom. There. On the toilet tank. The gun. Its pink skin was covered with fine beads of sweat. As though being left alone had made it tight with anxiety too. I toweled it dry. I warmed it against my chest. "This will not happen again," I assured it. But it remained reproachfully cold in my hand.

"Breaker-breaker." I spun around, my heart pumping. It was Control. I turned on all the water taps. I sat down on the toilet seat. Head between my knees. A darkness on the edge of things betrayed my fear. I knew what was coming. "You have been remiss, Sawtooth Tango." (A former code name; I cannot reveal my present designation. They get at you.)

"Breaker-breaker: But never again," I said. My voice, transmitted through cranial, dermal, gluteal circuitry, had a thin, watery sound to it.

"Breaker-breaker: In deep cover, once is too much."

The voice of Control died into the miniaturization of the bone implants. I turned off the water taps. I wiped my sweating neck on a towel. There was a scent on the towel I did not recognize. The cologne of Mr. Lewis?

I went back to the living room. On TV a man in combat fatigues was standing over a lamination of riddled bodies. "Take off your coat and stay awhile," Mr. Lewis said. "It's getting good."

"The coat stays on." In truth he annoyed me. "You'd better go home now, Mr. Lewis, or whatever your name is."

"Bill Lewis, fella. Your neighbor. And I think Elaine here wants me to stay."

Elaine was slabbed meat. The zombie pills coming on strong. She seemed to be watching TV. But the black slits of her eyes were lightless. "Get up," I said to Mr. Lewis.

"Get your finger out of my neck," he replied.

"It isn't my finger."

He tried to see what it was but couldn't. "Okay, I know when I've overstayed a welcome, fella."

"Good."

"And not too bad a welcome it was," he gibed.

I stabbed the belly gun deeper into his jowl. "I'm gone," he said.

He left. "He's gone," I said to Elaine.

"Who," she barely said.

"Our neighbor. Your friend. Your guest. Mr. Lewis."

"Bill."

I dropped it. "Bedtime, isn't it?" I suggested.

I helped her into the bedroom. The pills when they come on strong put her down for ten hours. I helped her undress. What tangles. I let her sit there on the bed with her bra around her neck and her dress on the floor around her thick ankles. I stood back from the sight. If I smiled she didn't see it.

I helped her into her nightgown. She wheezed down into the bed and began snoring. I yanked lightly on her hair. No, she was out. Asleep.

I went to the kitchen and removed the Master Plan from the freezing compartment of the fridge. They wouldn't look in there. Why would they? You know who. I thumbed it open to the Rs. Under Reckoning I read: "Be prepared. Readiness is our name. They have scheduled interferences to occur simultaneously. Communication lines will be useless. Use only subdermal, cranial, gluteal postmicrowave chip implants. Encode every word. Look again at those you trust most."

I went back into the bedroom and watched her sleep. But was it sleep? I yanked her hair again. But their discipline can be as good as ours. I imagine them saying everything I have been saying to you. With only minor differences. That is why you must not relax.

You must stay awake. You must learn to distrust the obvious. You must be ready for their first move. I am here to help you do this.

Queen

"**I**s it well done, is it cooked enough for you?" She looked over her shoulder at Page, who was seated at the table, chewing slowly, judging the meat. Evelyn looked over her shoulder again. "I asked, is it well done, is it cooked enough?" Her five cats were moving between her heavy ankles, coaxing her. She tested the large beet to see if it was done. Her legs were aching again. Page fished in his mouth, pulled out a torn piece of tendon. He wiped his fingers on his pants. He took another beer from the six-pack at his feet, removed the cap, drank deeply. Earlier she had annoyed him and he announced, "No, she's no mother, but she's a welfare queen just the same." He regretted saying it. He'd meant it as a joke and had snorted loudly in self-appreciation. Evelyn drank sweet port out of a water glass, and in the bar where he had said it, she began to cry. She put her face against Page's shoulder and moaned over and over, louder each time, and Page felt compelled to shrug hard against her face until she stopped it. Some at the bar smiled tolerantly, others bent to their drinks. She was near seventy and her heart was not good. The port, or sometimes the sherry, gave her strength. She was proud of her strong hands and she shook the hands of workingmen up and down the bar. She had good hands and liked to display them. The flesh was falling in her face and she was known as a character. She had never married. For years she had lived alone in a little house by the railroad bridge on the edge of Cutter Creek. The creek is full and green and explosive against big rocks in the spring, but by late summer it is nothing more than a trickle, studded with rusted cans. Evelyn looked over her shoulder and watched Page chewing slowly, reflectively. He was squinting, neck stiff, as he judged the meat. The hard veins in the backs of her knees ached. He had robbed her once, taking the welfare money, and she had forgiven him. It's all right, she had said, you needed it. He'd meant it as a joke, but he wound up spending it all. She tested the large beet to see if it was done. A log train carrying ponderosa made the small house jump. The dishes in the cupboard clattered. The train's slow rhythm rocked the floor. "Is it cooked enough for you?" Page searched the crevices of his teeth with his tongue, drank deeply from the tall brown bottle. He had regretted saying it, but the regret was dim in his mind now. He chewed the next piece of meat slowly, judging it. He said it again in the cab on the way home. "No, she's no mother. She's a queen, just the same." He left out the meanness this time. He left out the joke. He said it with tenderness, her head against his shoulder, her hand tightening on his. In the bar her hoarse sobbing was loud and inconsolable. It grew until the sly sound of death crept into it. He shrugged against her face until she stopped. Some in the bar smiled tolerantly. In the cab she whimpered demurely with an ageless femininity. She had dabbed her puffed eyes on a small silk hankie painted with wild flowers. She was much older than Page, who was only forty-three. They had been close friends for years and had seen happier days together before Evelyn's health had deteriorated. Page knew she could not live much longer. Her heart would often leave her legs and fingers numb and cramped with pain. It was on these occasions that she would coax Page to rub her feet and then her hands and arms. And Page would often agree, usually after explaining that he had some errands to run first, some people to see. Page had quit logging years ago. A tie chain on a lumber truck had snapped, splintering three vertebrae high in his back. The rolling rhythm of the log train sent a memory of pain into his neck. He knew he'd had to say it again in the cab, and said it firmly. Tenderly, but with masculine dignity. Earlier he'd meant it as a joke. The cabdriver had turned his head but not completely, then glanced in the rearview mirror. Page knew this would happen but he said it again, anyway. "No, she's no mother." Then he paused, making both the cabdriver and Evelyn stop to listen. Then he said, "But she's a queen just the same." Evelyn turned from the stove, her eyes swallowed by their surrounding flesh, her flesh sweating through the rosy makeup. "Is it well done, is it cooked enough?" Page's mouth was full. He swished the remaining beer until it was milky in the brown bottle. He glanced up at Evelyn, raised his eyebrows as if to speak, but only a soft belch murmured in his throat. He drank the remaining beer, giving moisture to the mass of meat and bread still in his mouth. Evelyn's five cats rubbed against her thick legs, some rising slightly, their pink mouths begging. He had taken her welfare money once, but she had forgiven him. You needed it, Page. It was a joke, he said. But he'd spent it all. She tested the large beet to see if it was done. Page fished in his mouth, pulled out a torn piece of tendon. In the cab she had said her legs were gone. The driver had looked back, impatient to end the afternoon shift. Page had watched her knuckles turn white against the hankie painted with yellow, blue, and purple wild flowers. Page said, "Ten years ago I was thirty-three." The cabdriver and Evelyn looked at Page. The slow meter ticked. The driver and Page helped Evelyn into the house. She was heavy with age and they entered sideways, the driver, Evelyn, then Page. They eased her down into the couch and she sank into its faded tapestry, sighing, then coughing. The sly sound of death creaked in her chest. Page paid the driver and the man left, letting the screen door slam. There had been an alarming moment for Page when Evelyn seemed lifeless. Her head was back on the couch. Her eyes were dim and fixed on distance. Page heard a thin rasping in her chest. He recalled the rasp of chain saws in the trees far away. Evelyn pushed a fork into the large beet. She looked over her shoulder at Page. Her cats rubbed against her legs, tails up and quivering. Page looked up from his food, squinting. He swished the remaining beer until it was milky in the brown bottle. He regretted saying it. He had never said anything like it before. And when Evelyn had asked him to do her legs he had said yes he would and that he had nothing else to do that was important. She looked up at him, the thin rasping in her breast gone, her pale eyes small and liquid. The stinging haze of chip burners was in the room. He knelt and removed her shoes. Her feet were splotched and swollen. The old toes yellowing. Evelyn leaned back into the faded tapestry and closed her eyes. Her face relaxed into an ageless femininity. It was the end of summer. The house retained the day's heat and would do so through the night. The thin ribbon of water called Cutter Creek made sly talking sounds against the large stones that lined its bed. The air was heavy and did not move. "I asked, is it well done, is it cooked enough for you?" Page searched the crevices of his teeth with his tongue. He squinted, his neck stiff, as he judged the meat. He drank the white beer. He regretted saying it. He'd never said anything like it before. And when she asked him to do her legs he said yes. His hands were hard with years of logging and he worked her veined calves with great gentleness. Evelyn leaned back into the stuffed cushions and closed her eyes. A chain saw somewhere rasped. She reached out and touched his head and her fingers went into his hair. She was proud of the strength in her hands. She had good hands and she liked to display them. She had shaken the hands of workingmen up and down the bar. She was known as a character. Some at the bar smiled tolerantly, some bent closer to their drinks. She closed her fingers on Page's hair and brought his face down slowly to her lap. Page made a soft murmuring sound. You're a sly one, she said, without anger. His neck was stiff. Evelyn looked over at Page, then tested the large beet to see if it was done. Her five cats rose between her legs, coaxing. Earlier he had said something he now regretted. Evelyn brought his face down slowly to her lap. Page gripped the backs of her knees and worked the hard knots of blue veins. Evelyn looked over her shoulder at Page. Page was seated at the table. He had robbed her once. It had been a joke. You're sly, she said. He fished in his mouth and pulled out a torn piece of tendon. She had good hands. She liked to display them. Her fingers moved willfully in his hair. He had never said anything like it before. It's all right, you needed it, she said. She looked over her shoulder at Page. Page glanced up. He swished the beer until it was milky. "Is it well done, is it cooked enough for you?"

Your Burden Is Lifted,
Love Returns

I lie on the nail-bed of my life still believing I am a good-hearted, sensitive man who would never beat his wife. You know my type: the afflicted, backsliding liberal, self-aware to a fault—narcissistic, my shrink would say—but above all, not a man who would pound on a woman with his fists.

I stood over my wife telling myself these things. Her lip was bleeding. She was sobbing silently into her hands, her shoulders lifting and falling in heartbreaking shudders. I looked at my still-smoking fist. It was hot and tingling with the shock of what it had done. *Was* it my fist? It looked alien. It was too big, too cabled with blue veins. The middle knuckle was red, the flesh dented and raw where it had scraped a tooth. It was the fist of the Brute: the blunt club-end of a Stone Age arm. I opened it and looked at the trembling fingers that had once stroked and probed the woman on the floor in the name of love and tender lust.

I looked at myself through the one-way glass of my tricky brain: I saw a stranger in the bedroom, unshaven, drunk in his underwear, the blood draining from his face as the enormity of what he has done begins to sink in.

He is a great fool.

He has just put his life on a steep downgrade slope and his brakes are questionable. He feels sick to his stomach; he wants to cry.

Raquel is sitting on the floor in her panties and bra, holding her mouth. The bedroom seems to dilate and contract in sympathy with her sobs. A line has been crossed in this marriage. Would it

be possible to pull it back to the other side? The mortified assailant
thinks not.

"You *hit* me," she says, rising, the nonchalant globes of her
breasts swinging, the wonderful curving flex of haunch and calf
reminding the fool of what has been forfeited here.

"You *hit* me," she repeats, unable to believe it herself. "You
bastard son of a *bitch!*"

"My God, Raquel, baby," he says, his heart a brick of remorse
in his unquiet chest.

"Do not use my name," she says: it is a careful instruction to
the humiliated beast. The intimate syllables are no longer his to
use. From this day forward, her name on his tongue will not be
her name. It will ring oddly in his ear, and though he will say it
over and over in tearful rages and in the half-sleep of early-morning
dreams, he won't be able to get it right.

Even her face is the face of a stranger. This is some random
woman, he thinks. A woman he might spy in Safeway fingering
the eggplant. He would appreciate her fine Latino profile, how it
hones itself with a shopper's glancing hesitations. Her eyes sharp
with intelligence and dark with explosive desire. This is a woman
he could love if he weren't already married to the woman he loves.
And she, of course, is happily married, too. She will not be picked
up in the produce section of Safeway like a common aisle-walking
tart. This last notion puts a wry twist on his lips and dilutes his
remorse with bile.

While he is occupied with this reverie, she kicks him. Her strong
foot rises up swiftly to his crotch, the instep impacting with a
rumpling thump. In his Jockey shorts, standing flatfooted before
her, he has offered a choice target of opportunity. He doubles over,
sick, and manages to get into the bathroom before he loses his
lamb chops, rice pilaf, and ratatouille. Not to mention the three
or four tumblers of Old Taylor.

"You *bastard!*" she howls, following him into the bathroom.
Her rage is on the upswing while his has peaked and dissipated.
Do not start fights if you cannot sustain your rage, he muses. He
is on his knees before the toilet, hugging the cool porcelain. Lemons
of sick light float before his shut eyes.

"I think I'm hurt bad," he manages to say between convulsions.

"Not bad enough," he hears her whisper. He notices that her breath is choppy. He imagines that a dangerous wind has blown open the house, that she is teetering in it, holding on to a wall for support. He sees her hair standing out from her head, her eyes wild. Rags of rage snap in this insane wind. He sees the house lifted off its foundation, transferred by storm to a country without maps.

Then she touches his shoulder. He almost sobs aloud with gratitude. But it is not a forgiving hand. It is her foot again. (The foot he has kissed and tickled.) This time it shoves him into the toilet tank. His head gongs off the hard surface. A thread of blood weaves itself into his philosophic eyebrows.

By the time he has cleaned himself up and stopped the oozing blood from the hairline laceration, Raquel has dressed and packed her suitcase.

"Don't go," he says. "I think I have a concussion."

"Fine," she says briskly. "Perhaps in the future you will use your head more wisely."

"You won't find a motel this time of night," he informs her.

"I'll sleep in the car, then," she says, snapping the locks on her suitcase.

"Or maybe not," he says, alluding to the subject that had put the evening's events into suicidal fast-forward.

"I am not going to dignify that sick remark with an answer," she says.

Sick remarks, he thinks, *have become my specialty.* He tries to reconstruct the last three hours. It seems more like days than hours. He, the responsible house husband, is out of sorts. Raquel, the breadwinner, has come home late and dinner is cold on the table. He could have kept it warm in the oven, but the cold and coagulated dinner makes a better *statement.* He is being spiteful. Spite: the bitter pill that spoils love's slim chances. It hardens the soft core of stumblebums and statesmen alike. Spite: the great rotten god with baleful glance who systematically unravels the good world.

Through the smoked glass of memory, he watches his fist floating toward her. It seems, at first, that it only wants to deliver a semi-playful chuck under the chin. But he is grossly self-deceived. (Because of self-deception and spite, he sees little hope for the human race.) The fist has energy and hidden purpose. It is not as playful as he thought it was. Her lip cracked. A tooth stung his knuckle. She sat down.

Earlier he received her explanation with an indifference he almost believed. But it was spite again, masking itself with reason, mocking reason's coolness with sub-zero rage.

"Oh, *no*, honey," she said. "Look, it's past *eight*. I didn't realize . . . I'm really sorry, but—"

He turned his back on her then and mixed himself a drink. Bourbon, because he knew she detested the smell.

"Doug Thurston called a supervisory meeting because of the pothole crisis in the South End," she said. "I had to take the notes."

"Until eight?" he said mildly, speaking into his glass.

"Well, no, not until eight. We finished at six-thirty. But Doug—"

"Doug?"

"Mr. Thurston. He wanted to buy me . . . *us*, I mean . . . a drink. You know, for being good sports. The secretaries."

"Where did you go?"

"The Yucatan Room, at the Sheraton. Lowell Black was there, and Mary and Charlene. They want me to play racquetball with them. Mary Tyson had to drop out because of shin splints. So their foursome is shot."

"I'm sorry . . . ?" he said, setting his glass down carefully, his brow creased with the mock-sincere but game effort to understand her.

"But I told them I'm not the racquetball type."

"What type did you tell them you were?"

Raquel searched his face for the possible joke, but his face was neutral. His intentions were hidden, even from himself.

"You could have called me," he said, still without rancor.

"I know, I know, hon," she said indulgently. "I *should* have called. I just lost track, you know? And Doug—"

"*Doug?*"

"Mr. Thurston, the boss. Doug Thurston. He wanted to make it up to us." She gave him a small pecking kiss on the ear, notable for its motherliness and parceled heat. He clenched his jaw against it, and against the thing that was trying to surface in his mind.

He smelled, then, the tequila sunrises, the barroom smoke, the cologne of self-important bureaucrats. He felt rocked back by those essences. "God damn it," he said, convinced of the awful thing that had been skirting his thoughts the past few hours. For this was not the first time Raquel had come home late from her job at the Department of Streets. Once last week, twice the week before, and several times the previous month.

She looked at him, her head cocked inquisitively, like an alerted robin sensing the stalking cat. She heard the octave difference in his shaky voice as events began their sickening climb toward the blooded summit. "What's wrong, honey?" she said.

He finished his drink in a single corrosive gulp and set the glass down with a slam that startled both of them. "Wrong?" he said. "Nothing's wrong. What makes you think something's wrong?" Yet all this insistent innocence was betrayed by the tremors in his voice.

"I—"

He cut her off: "Let's eat this slop before it walks off the table."

He picked up the plates and put them into the microwave, hers first, then his. The food came out gummy but warm, and they sat down to their evening meal. Since he had been out of work, he'd become a passable if somewhat paranoid cook. If praise wasn't forthcoming after the first or second bite, he was thrown into a grievous sulk.

After dinner he went back to the Old Taylor. Bourbon pacified him, oddly. He became more civil as the evening progressed. She went on about racquetball, about how great Mary and Sally were (he was not clear who these women were—secretaries, apparently, but Raquel seemed to be flattered to find herself in their company), what a great boss Doug Thurston was, how he had promised to consider her for the next opening at the Administrative Assistant level, and so on. He began to feel, gradually, like a ball of string being unwound at the hand of an idiot child, even though the bourbon helped him maintain the illusion of solidity. While Raquel spoke, he touched himself surreptitiously a few times to see if he was still there. Yes, yes, his body seemed to say, we are still here, all of us: meat, bone, gristle, blood, marrow, the beating, secreting, and pumping organs, the wiring and plumbing, all present and accounted for. As it was in the beginning, so is it now, and so shall it be at the end of time. The false alpha and omega wisdom of bourbon, storming through his tender corpus, led these wacky musings. But there were always the tricyclic antidepressants to help him through the day-after black-hole blues.

"I'm sorry, I missed that last thing you said," he confessed, suppressing, now, a smile that he knew would be hellishly dashing if he let it break out.

"*Tomorrow*, I said. I'll be working late again, so you might as well cook only for one. Or maybe you can go to a restaurant. I'll give you an extra ten dollars."

"Oh, yes," he said. "That will be fine."

He managed to sit through three back-to-back sitcoms. He listened to Raquel's tinkling, careless laughter as Bob Newhart's stammering attempts to claim patriarchal authority elicited gales of laughter from the audience. He hated Bob Newhart suddenly, recognizing himself, and half the men he knew, in that beaten, paunchy little guy: twerps, nerds, schlepps, and all the unremarkable cuckolds—*cabrones,* Raquel would say if moved to Hispanic cruelty—portrayed so perfectly by the Everyman for our times, Bob Newhart. It occurred to him that if the sitcoms were uncensored, if commercial considerations were not a factor, and if the writers were given a free hand, then we would see ourselves as no dramatic literature has ever made any nation see itself. What the Newhart show needed was one more twist toward the black end of the spectrum. A little manic wobble to worry its too-tidy spin.

Raquel was laughing lightly at Newhart, who once again was left holding the bag. She laughed, too, at the troop of fools who complicated his life, while the women moved handily toward the things they wanted, unimpeded.

"God *damn* it," he said later, when they were undressing for bed, in answer to no remark but to an image in his mind of Newhart standing in a snowbank outside his lodge so that he could peek into a window to spy on his wife. Inside, by the fire, she was allowing an insurance adjuster to pat and paw her, hoping to get a higher estimate on a claim. It was vital to Bob that she succeed, though her sheer skill made him bite his knuckles.

"What?" Raquel said, unable or unwilling to acknowledge the gripe that had quietly soured the evening.

"You're sleeping with him, aren't you?" he said. "You're sleeping with Doug."

"*Doug?*"

"Doug Thurston. Your boss."

"*What?* Are you crazy? Did you take your medication today?"

This made him laugh. He approached her. "My medi*cation?* Is *that* what I need? Get the hubby zonked, then everyone's free to play? Is that the way it works?"

"You are being an incredible asshole, you know that, don't you?"

"Just answer the question, Raquel. Are you sleeping with Doug or not?"

Her eyes flashed in that Latin way he was crazy about. It opened glandular spigots everywhere. It made his hair flex. "Okay, sure. I'm sleeping with him. Is that what you want to hear? Does that thrill you a lot? I'm sleeping with him two, three times a day. In his office, in the janitor's closet, out in his Mercedes. The Mercedes is best, all that leather and the stereo system . . ."

Denial by exaggeration, as a technique, bored him. He laughed again. His laugh was dry and weak, as though his vocal cords were made of paper. He felt an itch in his right hand. The itch made the hand curl into a fist. He thought of giving her a little "chuck" under the chin. But his glandular spigots had been opened wide, amplifying the gesture: the chuck had steam.

I didn't sleep that night. Or the next. I took my medication but that didn't bring her back. I called Doug Thurston. Raquel hadn't been to work for two days. (He said.)

I called my shrink, but he had flown his Piper Cherokee to Alaska to videotape caribou migration. Several times I found myself standing in the bathroom with large quantities of pills in my willful hand: cloud-gray bullets, tiny disks the tired pink of haze-dampened suns. On these occasions I became afraid of the unshaven stranger in the mirror.

I took refuge in chores. I cleaned the house to showplace perfection. I resumed half-finished projects—the windows needed caulking, the patio slab needed paint. While rolling a new layer of insulation across the attic, I found a newspaper dated March 15, 1949. The quaint headlines amused me for a while. The world of thirty-eight years ago seemed only *knee*-deep in quicksand. It was up to its armpits now, praying for a rope. My horoscope was short and sweet: "Your burden is lifted, love returns." I took it to heart. In the mantic arts, thirty-eight-year discrepancies are trifles only the literal-minded take seriously.

It was a pleasant day, sunny with promise. I took a six-pack of beer out to the front porch and waited for her.

Red Chair

The chair appeared in her room one morning as if it had grown out of the carpet overnight. Had she asked for it? She doubted that very much. It was ugly. She hated it. It was far too big for her room, and not only too big, it was *red*. She hated red. Red was Arizona. Red was New Mexico. And this was a red that glistened. Light from the window danced and flashed in a hundred vinyl panes so that the chair seemed to be emitting a cold, hellish fire. She got out of bed and walked over to it, reaching out gingerly with shaking hands as though to ward off the offensive glare. Then the smell struck her, like a fetid wind, and she staggered. It was the cold smell of new plastic, but it reminded her of something else, something kept in a dark, wet place.

Her room could not accommodate red. Her room was soft and small, done mostly in browns and greens. No glassy splinters of light were welcome here. No arrogant reds. She turned away and closed her eyes, but she could not make the image of the chair go away. She visualized against her will, the unnatural glistening of the chair's high red back. It made the bones of her forehead ache, and she could feel its cold weight distort the room. It was massive, a recliner, and she imagined the floor tilting in its direction. And then she actually felt the floor under her feet *tilt*. She slid toward the chair, her slippers skidding on the waxed tiles—a vertigo attack, she knew, but it was as if the chair had taken possession of her room and now sought to take control of her, too. She cried out and opened her eyes and faced the chair again. It glowed like a spiteful thing in the morning light. And now it seemed like a yawning red mouth, sucking her toward it, wanting her, its dank plastic smell heavy in the room. She pulled her afghan off the bed and threw it over the chair, but the afghan wouldn't hold to the slippery surface. It bunched up into itself and tumbled to the floor.

She compressed her lips and narrowed her eyes. It was a look she reserved for hateful things. Often in her life she had wished for the nerve to turn this look on certain people. It was a private look meant to wither its recipient, but given only to inanimate things or to contemptible people in their absence. Her head began to oscillate from side to side, minutely, as if to underscore a decisive and final No. It was an unyielding denial, final and absolute. It was not a momentary gesture, half meant, done and forgotten, but an enduring habit. It went on long after its reasons were gone. It went on during her knitting, when her mind drifted from one thing to another. Sometimes her husband had watched this negative rocking of her head even after she seemed asleep. It annoyed him. They were younger then, but he was not going to live much longer. He departed when he was only fifty-five. Heart. Arteries. "Why do you insist on doing that, Mary?" he had asked. Bart was a hard man to aggravate. He would stay silent through most things he didn't approve of. Like the time the city claimed an unreasonable easement and removed his roses bordering the sidewalk. But her head-rocking made him speak out. Her children noticed it, too, but they were grown by then and never mentioned it to her. Side to side, rapid as the heartbeat of an infant, a denial from the insensible marrow of personality.

The soft colors of her room had been her choice. Other rooms were done in yellows, pinks, and blues. These were called the Californias. Others, called the Arizonas and New Mexicos, were done in terra-cotta, fiery orange, gypsum white. Hers was a Wisconsin. The large picture that filled half the wall above the simulated hearth had been painted especially for the Wisconsins. Browns and soft yellows, greens dying away into fall, a heavy zinc sky, the buried sun, dark red barns, blond fields, animals, children running toward home, their straw hats a-kilter, a low house down by the dark river, its windows brimming with a welcoming warm and buttery light. The painting was like the manifestation of a real memory, and she thought of the scene as her actual home.

The red chair had been put in her room while she had been in Activities. Everyone got a brand-new recliner. They were all red, all slippery, all huge, dominating presences. The chairs had been a charitable gift from a service club. The club—Lions, Eagles, Moose, perhaps Elks—had taken advantage of a closeout sale. Red was not a successful color for recliners. The club had bought sixty-one of these chairs at a fraction of their retail price. They were quality chairs, massive, well made, with solid oak frames. There had been a surprise announcement, but she had forgotten about it. The president of the service club had presented Tom Banning, the Director, with a framed bill of sale. The president of the club then made a speech. "Our wonderful seniors," he had said, "grand grand people to whom we owe so much, for they are the soil in which this country grew." She remembered the occasion, the speech, but did not connect it to the surprise arrival of the chair.

After the club president finished his speech, Tom Banning made a hearty, scooping gesture with his hands, lifting the air in front of him and tossing it up and over his shoulders with wonderful vigor. It was the signal for applause. During Glee Club or Memory Game he gave this signal often. He did it at the Christmas party when costumed as Santa Claus and then everyone knew right away it was only Tom Banning behind the beard and pillow-stuffed stomach. "We know it's you, Tom Banning!" someone would shout, and Tom would do an odd, tiptoe dance, feinting in and out of the crowd, his small black eyes animal bright under his shaggy black eyebrows. This would make everyone laugh. Everyone liked Tom. He had pep and could make you laugh when you believed you'd never want to laugh again. And best of all, he wasn't too young for the job. The previous Director had been forty. Forty is too young. Forty is a pup. A Director only forty will say things. Such as: Everybody's in the same leaky boat here, Miss Mary. Why do you think your problems are so special? Or: Are we crying in our beer again, sweetheart? Are we feeling sorry for ourselves? Step lively, Miss Mary! Mary, you look like *Death Eating a Cracker!*

Mary, Mary, do you mean to say you came into my office during the busiest time of day to tell me *that?* Tell it to *Hap,* Mary. A Director only forty will sit behind his desk like a Captain of Industry and put his hands behind his head and stare at something above your head and grin like a mustachioed bandit when there's no call for it whatever. *Tell it to Hap,* he will say, with a mean grin on his lips. You want to give him a look that puts him squarely in his place, but you won't think of it until you're back in your room searching the radio dial for Hap, or when you're in Activities when it's too late.

She tried to push the chair into a corner. It was far too big where it was, in front of the TV set, practically in the middle of the room. But it would not move and the effort made her dizzy. Dazzling blue spots of light, like fragments of sky, floated in front of her eyes, so real that she tried to brush them aside. Her breath was fast and high up in her chest, as if the air could not reach down into her lungs. She turned the TV set on and leaned on it. The Christian channel came on and Polly Reem was there, *The Morning Hour of Victory,* a program she rarely missed. "I tell you true, whatever your station in life, help is on the way, but only if you accept the Lord into your heart," Polly said. Polly closed her eyes and held the flat of her hand out to the television audience. The red chair, minified in the convex television screen, sat like a fiendish joke in the evangelist's hand.

Tom Banning led the three-wheel-bike excursion to the park. He yelled boisterous instructions over his shoulder through a bullhorn. It had rained for several days and the toadstools were up in great numbers. Mary rode next to Carl Simpson and Betty Morris. Tom Banning's amplified voice sliced over their heads. Its thin, electrical edge made her ears ring. "Yes! I see a great Violet Rider!" Tom shouted. His voice struck her ears like wind with sand in it. "All dismount! All dismount! Let's have a look!"

Everyone braked his three-wheeler and dismounted carefully. Tom Banning strode off into the trees. The others formed a ragged line and followed stiffly. They could not keep pace with the Director, who loved nature trips. Tom Banning was proud of his physical condition. It was well known that he was over sixty-five, but he looked fifty, even forty-five. He had black hair and full sideburns touched with white. He wore a trim mustache and an arrowhead of chin whiskers. His long strides carried him into the trees and out of view. Only his enthusiastic shouts over the bullhorn kept his followers informed of his whereabouts. "Veer off to your left when you reach the live oak!" said the Director, his voice seeming to come from the tops of the trees. "Then cross the meadow! This way! This way! You won't get lost! I see Fairy Rings! I see giant Puffballs!"

Mary wasn't interested in toadstools. She held Betty Morris back. They sat down on a dry bench. Mary sat twisting her ring. She saw that Betty was watching her do this. She left the stone facing haphazardly to one side and adjusted her sweater around her neck. The afternoon was rich with humus and rain. A large black dog trotted past their bench, its paws clicking on the asphalt path. It regarded the two old women indifferently, then began sniffing their bikes. It lifted a leg.

"Do you like your chair?" Mary asked.

"The new chairs?"

"The red one."

"The recliners, to watch TV in?"

"I guess that's what they're for."

"Oh, it's wonderful!"

"But it's so big," Mary insisted.

"Well, yes, it *is* big. I slept on mine last night."

"Oh, no, you couldn't have!"

"I didn't mean to. I was watching the late movie. Then Tom came by. He's so funny. He said, Betty have you tried the massager? I didn't know what in the world he was talking about. But listen, you can plug the chair into an outlet and it massages you, with heat, too, if you want it. Tom said, Betty, it will make you feel *younger*."

Mary narrowed her eyes. The pressure from her compressed lips made her nostrils turn white and flare. Betty fidgeted. Mary made the stone on her finger revolve fast as a beacon. But Betty Morris was her friend. They had been new together five years ago and had sought each other's company. "That *dog*," Mary said, giving false direction to her disgust. She shook her head and then the shaking did not stop. "Shoo, you bad pup," she scolded, her head rocking. "Go *on!*"

Tom Banning came striding out of the trees, his arms loaded with several varieties of toadstools. The others straggled after him. He spread the toadstools out on the grass and motioned the crowd to form a circle around them. Then he did his odd little tiptoe dance, feinting in and out of the crowd. He held two fingers upright at his forehead and made grunting sounds. "Stag of the woods!" he roared. "Stag of the woods!"

Everyone laughed, enjoying Tom's antics. He seemed so young, so full of life. "The chef's delight!" he said, indicating the toadstools. "But say, you have got to be careful. You have got to know what you're doing. This little character, for instance," he said, holding up a small toadstool, "this little guy is called *Amanita verna,* or, in everyday parlance, the Destroying Angel. Don't eat it! Don't even touch it! Leave-it-where-it-lies! But these little old puffballs and fairy rings and boletus are the gourmet's best friends."

Mary, Betty, and Carl Simpson stood closest to Tom Banning. Tom was sweating profusely, even though the air was chilly. His breath made humble complaints as it raked over his vocal cords. He broke open a puffball with his big, soiled thumbs and showed everyone the rich white flesh.

"What's the difference between a toadstool and a mushroom?" Carl Simpson asked.

"No difference!" Tom said. " 'Toadstool' comes from the German, meaning 'death stool' or 'chair of death.' So we generally prefer to use the word 'mushroom.' "

" 'Chair of death'?" Mary said. "I don't think that's right."

Tom looked at her oddly, his small black eyes sharply focused. He stood up to his full height and filled his lungs gradually, as if setting himself for an ordeal, but all he said was "Me oh my."

"Why do they call them a fungus, Tom?" someone asked.

"Well, that's precisely what they are," Tom said, as if miffed by the question. "They're parasites, incapable of making their own food."

"How's that, Tom?"

"I mean it! They don't have chlorophyll, you see. They don't make their own food through photosynthesis, like other plants do, and so they need to sponge off a host."

"Welfare bums," someone said.

Tom laughed and did his little tiptoe dance.

Everyone appreciated Tom Banning's energy. It seemed boundless at times, and almost unnatural for a man of his age. *How does he do it?* was a common question, often heard after Activities. Once Tom had made a brief, solemn speech about his philosophy. "I don't believe in old age," he said. This was shortly after he was hired as Director. "I do not accept it. I do not accept it in myself, and therefore I will not accept it in you. You are as young as you feel, and my job, as I see it, is to make you folks feel *good*."

Tom packed the toadstools into the saddlebags on his bike, and then they all cycled back. They had to switch on their headlights because the sky had darkened with rain clouds again. Several of the riders were coughing. Tom sang, "Pack up your troubles in your old kit bag and smile, smile, smile," into his bullhorn, using only one hand to guide his bike.

At dinner, Carl Simpson said, "Ah, darn, my bursitis." He touched the point of his shoulder with the tips of his fingers. He winced and pursed his lips.

"It's that chair," Mary said.

"Chair?" Carl said.

"The new red ones. They're cold to the touch. You can't cover it either. It's too slippery."

"No," Carl said, rotating his right arm carefully. "It was the bike ride. The air was damp. Didn't you notice how damp the air got?"

"It *was* damp, Carl," Betty Morris agreed.

Someone at the next table leaned toward them and said, "That bike ride give you an ache, too?"

"You bet!" Carl said, still rotating his arm at the shoulder.

"It's the chair," Mary said, compressing her lips and narrowing her eyes, apparently at her food. She put her fork down. It rang against her plate. She pushed away from the table and stood up.

"What's she so burned up about?" Carl asked, after Mary had left the dining room. "Look, she didn't touch her food."

Betty shrugged. "She doesn't like how they spice meat loaf."

Carl scoffed loudly. "Tell it to Hap, Mary," he said, bending to his food. Betty smiled knowingly.

Mary didn't come out for Memory Game that evening. She was tired of trying to put together dates and faces with events. She wasn't as good at it as the others. The men excelled. The date is 1934. This is the face. Who can tell me what the momentous event was? One of the men would always catch Tom's eye and shout out the answer and Tom would hoot and dance on his toes. The Social Security Act, Tom! The Tennessee Valley Authority, Tom! Hey, isn't that Bing Crosby? Der Bingle himself, Tom? The women didn't like to compete with the shouting men. They were content to do their knitting or needlework as the men tried to outdo each other. Mary scored a point only once. The men were stumped. The "It" girl, she said. Clara Bow. Tom scooped the air in front of him over both shoulders and got everyone to give Mary a big hand.

When she was readying herself for bed later that night, Tom Banning knocked on her door and opened it a crack before she had a chance to answer. "It's only me," he said. "Might I come in for a moment?"

She thought she would say no, but she said yes and he pushed the door all the way open. "Betty tells me you don't understand your chair, Mary," he said. He was in his pajamas and robe. His robe was scarlet with an animal of some kind embroidered above the right breast. A lion, perhaps, with eagle wings.

"I'm waiting for Hap," she said, cautioning him not to stay long.

"I'll only be a minute," he said.

In his pajamas and robe, in the small light from her bed lamp, Tom Banning didn't seem so large and vigorous. His hair, she noticed, was much thinner than it appeared in daylight. His flesh, too, seemed to sag. There were dark gray half-moons under his eyes. The flesh around his mouth was loose and she realized that his teeth were false and that he was not wearing them.

He knelt down on the floor and crawled behind the chair. He felt around under it and then held up an electrical plug. "Hah, you see!" he said, offering her a pink-gum smile of triumph. "You didn't plug it in, either! You can't get full benefit unless it is plugged in, Mary." He pulled himself up with a groan and stood next to her, his round belly touching her. "Now, climb in and I'll show you how to operate it."

"No, I'm—"

"It'll only take a minute. You owe it to yourself, Mary. You'll feel a hundred percent after an hour in this beauty."

He put his arm around her waist and moved her toward the chair. Then he turned her around so that the backs of her legs were against the red cushion. She had no choice but to sit, and when she was seated Tom moved a lever and the chair fell back into its fully reclined position, taking Mary down with it. Her vertigo came on strong with the sudden movement. She began an endless fall, the chair falling under her. Tom pressed some buttons under the arm of the chair and devices in the cushions began to hum. Gradual heat penetrated the small of her back, then traveled up her spine. Something in the chair moved against her flesh. It felt like large, soft knuckles urging her impatiently to answer some unstated question.

"Tell me you're not comfortable," Tom said. "This is state-of-the-art comfort, Mary."

Tom helped her out of the chair. She held his hand harder than she wanted to, but she was still dizzy.

"It's tough, I know," Tom said, misunderstanding the pressure of her hand. "You gals miss some big lug lounging around the house, the old handyman taking care of things. Sure, they smell up a place with beer and smoke, but they get things done."

"What are you talking about?" Mary said.

"Don't kid me, Mary." He put his hands on her shoulders and squeezed. He rocked her a little so that she had to put one foot behind the other.

"Get out."

"I don't believe in old age. I do not accept it, Mary."

"Get out of here, you fool," she said.

Tom Banning's face fell into a diagonal grin, one side of his mouth up, the other down. "Another time," he said, winking.

After closing and locking the door behind Tom, Mary went to bed. The chair in the soft light from her bed lamp looked like a wet piece of freshly cleavered meat. Its redness was leaky now. It spread. The walls of the room, and the ceiling, took on a reddish stain. The Wisconsin pastels were mottled with red. When she turned the bed lamp out, she could smell it. A dank, underground smell, more like a cold dirt-wall basement than brand-new plastic. Vertiginous again, she felt herself slipping easily down a ramp into such a basement. She turned the lamp on again, to dispel the dizziness, and the chair throbbed into being. She put her hand to her mouth and whimpered, for the chair had seemed, in that first pulse of light, like a crouching burglar, contemptuous of discovery.

She turned on the radio. The Hap Wilcox show was on at last. It was a call-in show, and it was like having company you didn't have to tidy up for. You could lie in your robe, close your eyes, and let your thoughts travel, carried by distant voices. Hap Wilcox was a pleasant young man who had made a career out of listening to the problems of the elderly. For someone so young he seemed to have a special understanding. Most of the callers were from other Homes around the state. Some of the Homes were as far north as Fresno and Sacramento. A bedridden man named Everett had talked for half an hour all the way from Bend, Oregon.

"Yes, dear," Hap was saying. "Yes, it *is* a shame. No question. I totally agree. I do. Bye-bye now, Emily. Give our love to Dottie."

Mary placed her call and put the phone down next to her pillow. You had to wait your turn, that was the only trouble. Sometimes it was only fifteen minutes, sometimes twice that.

At first she thought the voices were another radio station in the background, a crowd of well-wishers seeing someone off on an ocean voyage. But there was a darker sound, like a mob of people kneeling in rows, praying. She turned the radio down and the voices remained, but they weren't really voices. It was the chair. Tom had forgotten to turn it off. The machinery inside the upholstery was still turning, still massaging, though the chair was empty. A grumbling, murmurous sound, repeating a meaningless cycle of complaint. She turned the radio up again. There was a commercial on, a man whose voice she'd heard before, possibly on television, praising a prepaid funeral service called The Forever-After Plan.

Mary dozed off as the silky voice went on and on. Her short dream was vivid but meaningless and she woke to her name, *Mary, Mary,* being called by a chorus, a muddy chorus, dark and shameful, somewhere, and it was then she realized she hadn't awakened but was still dreaming. She woke herself through small panic and an effort of will.

"And they never take it *out,* Hap," said a weeping voice. "They leave it in the halls until it stinks. Hap, it just is not sanitary!"

"I totally agree, Viv. It's a shame, it really is," said Hap.

"It's just like garbage."

"I understand. Yes, I see that, Viv."

"Do you see what I mean, Hap?"

"Honey, I'd have to be blind to miss it. Listen, you raise the dickens with them. Remember my motto: Face trouble head-on. Don't shrink from a fight. They want you to back down, Viv. They'd like to see you quit."

"Oh, Hap, you're so wonderful."

"Not at all. I call 'em like I see 'em, hon."

The *Mary, Mary*—the voice was muffled, the mouth stuffed with wet rags—was rising from the chair. She knew it was only her imagination, sparked by the dream, and she could have easily made herself hear something else (for it was like the sound a river makes, the low, watery voices calling one's name, or murmuring endlessly the many names of creation, as she often imagined rivers doing when she was a child), but it was an effort she did not want to make.

Then a powerful ringing sound pierced all the other sounds. "Who do we have here?" Hap was saying under the screech.

Mary picked up her phone. "Am I on?" she asked.

"No, *no.* This won't do. You have to turn your radio down. *Turn-it-down.*"

"Oh, yes. Hello, Hap? Am I on? It's Mary. It's just me, Mary again."

"Hi, *Mary,*" Hap said at last. "Is that really you, darling?"

Mary swallowed against a thickening in her throat. "Yes, it's me," she said. "It's me again, Hap."

"Hi, lover. What's on your mind *tonight?*"

"Oh, Hap."

"I'm right here, babe. Don't be hard to get, hon. Are they treating you all right?"

"I'm such a pest, Hap."

"No way, dear. Not at all. I won't have that, Mary."

"Maybe I'm just a complaining old woman."

"Hey, I'm going to have to scold you, Mary. *Old* woman is a definite no-no on my show. Old *man,* too, guys. Okay? Are we clear on that, gang? These are the Hap Wilcox ground rules."

"You're so good to me, Hap," Mary said.

"I am not. I'm a filthy young man, a total swine. Now, let's not blow all our time on pleasantries. What's on your mind tonight, darling?"

There were many things on her mind, a lifetime's accumulation, but now they lost their old arbitrary boundaries and merged into a specific thing of suffocating weight.

"I can't *hear* you, babes. Is there someone there with you? Are you compromised?"

Mary shut her eyes against the solemn murmurs of the red chair. She concentrated hard on Hap's voice. ("Come *on,* don't be a tease," it was saying.)

Medicine Man

*L*ouis Quenon can make you feel better than you had any right to expect. You'll hear it said he's trouble in the long run. You'll hear it said he'll drink a week and disappear for two. They'll tell you he's a Feejee Indian from Africa. They'll call him a breed, oily customer, quack, boomer, con man, crook. Someone will get around to telling you he was born in a canebrake on the Guadalupe ten miles below Duck Pond, and a lot of other fairy tales. His wife, Lily, will tell you he's irresponsible and doesn't care what becomes of her in this life or the next. "You morons!" she yells at us. We'll be sitting there with him in Lucky's, drinking beer or sweet wine, listening. Lily will come in, a hard, narrow-hipped, bony woman of fifty. She'll start in swinging her big red purse, knocking glasses and pitchers to the floor. Louis looks at her as you might look at a waxwing mindlessly hurting itself against a plate-glass window. "Useless old drunks!" she yells. "Stupid *re*tards!" We all scatter to the dark corners of the bar, except for Louis, and wait for the storm to blow over. Louis takes his time. He has the patience of a mountain, whatever else they might say. He lights up a cigarette. He arranges his lighter and tobacco pouch on the table neatly before him. He asks Leonard, the bartender, who's winning the ball game. He tilts his chair back. He looks up at the TV set as if at the blue sky. His smile has never had any meanness in it. He looks at Lily. Her anger, which was a solid brick wall coming in, is now like a flimsy membrane thinning out and getting weaker, yielding to a stretching force in the air. Louis will pat the table, rub his stomach or stick a wood match in his ear for wax, and Lily's temper will come to heel, snap, and it's gone. Louis beams. He takes her by the wrist, easy, and she sits down, shaking her head at her own bad manners, but feeling a whole lot better. Louis makes a sign to Leonard and everyone in the bar resumes his conversation and drinking. The incident is forgotten. Someone will usually dump a load of quarters in the jukebox, and everything is back to normal.

Now, this is what you *won't* hear: Louis Quenon was a real medic in the U.S. Army. He saw action in Sicily and North Africa. He got to know the local herb doctors and practitioners of antique medicine. They showed him things they usually never showed to outsiders. They warned him against surgery directed against the major organs, indecision, and a generally unrecognized plague they called, in a half-joking way, "glitter-blindness." He ran across a cell of modern Pythagoreans who claimed the universe was nothing more than an idea about tight bundles of woven lines. He who masters the art of line-bundling geometry, they said, will see the Weaver's Hand. When he returned to the States, Louis refused a scholarship to a big midwestern university that he had won in an open competition. In his letter turning down the offer, he said: "Dear Dean, This is to let you know that I've had second thoughts after reading through your catalog and that you are probably barking up the wrong tree over there in Madison."

His tribal name is Then-He-Sees-It, but he is only a fraction Assiniboin. His great-uncle, Willard Quenon, was a medicine man and they say that's where his talent comes from. But Louis says no to all of that, insisting that what he knows comes from a marabout he got acquainted with in Marrakech, and from the Sicilian herb specialists. What his Indian uncle Willard knew worked pretty well among the Tribe, but Louis said it wasn't very effective with white people. For the white man's diseases, you've got to go to the roots of the old white world and find the ancient remedies.

He cured me of a delicate constitution with a snail-water recipe that is still widely used in southern Europe by rural people. That's how I met Louis. We were at the bar, in Lucky's, accidentally sitting next to each other. He's a big, heavy man with a wide Indian face but his hair is blond and he has a full beard that scratches against his chest. Our eyes met in the mirror behind the bottles. "How long have you had these fainting spells?" he asked me. Right off, my heart did its butterfly imitation and the barroom tilted.

"How did you know about that?" I said, short of breath.

"You write this down," he said.

I started to slide off my stool, but Louis touched my arm and that stopped me. I borrowed a pencil from Leonard and wrote down what Louis said on a paper napkin. Here's what put me back on my feet:

"A fourth bushel of good garden snails," he said. "Put them in a deep clay pot and lay some mint on top of them along with some balm and fennel to clean them. Let them stand all night like that with a colander over them so they can't creep out. In the morning wipe them one by one with a clean cloth and then bruise the snails, shells and all, into a fine mortar. Mix this mortar into six quarts of red cow's milk and set it on a medium fire, stirring all the while until it is thick as cream. Have a big pot ready. Lay a double handful of mint, half as much pennyroyal, ale hoof, and hyssop, then pour in the mixture. After two hours on a high flame stir it up or else it will scum on top. When it cools off some, but before the pot gets comfortable to the touch, put it into as many Mason jars of any size as the mixture will fill. Put three ounces of white sugar candy in the bottom of each jar to kill the taste."

I had a hard time admitting to myself that I wanted to find those ingredients, and a lot harder time actually finding them. But I did, and right away, after the first quart or so, I began to take on color. In six months' time I'd gained thirty pounds. My lungs began to take in more air than they'd ever been able to, and my heart felt like a big fist opening and closing. I moved out of my small room above Lucky's and rented a little three-room house outside of town and put in a big garden where I could grow the hard-to-find herbs along with a good variety of greens. I felt like a healthy man of forty-five, and I'd been on a railroad pension for several years.

There's always a table or booth at Lucky's with a crowd of us believers trading stories. The younger customers, of course, think we're a bunch of senile old fools. They think Louis is a common type of gyppo artist, although he's never asked one of us for money, help, or goods. No one ever asks him why he offers to pass on a cure to ailing folks because the question won't come up. You'll be sitting there, telling stories, adding a few frills here and an outright lie there, held in place by a common denominator of unswerving belief:

"You remember that black spot on my neck? Well, it got big and began to spread out like a stain. When it was as big as a dollar, I went to Louis. He gave me this yellow paste that smelled like antelope musk and in a week it went back to normal."

"I couldn't put any weight on my right leg. Louis said the big vein was shutting down. He gave me a blue unguent. Now I can dance all night."

"I was growing what I took to be a sixth finger."

"My left ear had a bell in it."

"I'd wake up every other night hollering for my brother, who drowned when he was only three."

"The wife thought the lead slipped out of my pencil fifteen years ago."

"My eyes were turning into bone."

"I'd sit down to grunt and nothing would come out but this nasty blue twine. I'd have to cut it off and hope for better luck tomorrow."

Here's another one. They took Moley Gleeson to the county hospital in a taxi. Moley had the room next to mine on the second floor above Lucky's. This was about a month before I moved out. I'd heard him blubber. I went into his room and found him sitting on the john, shaking with a chill and biting his hands. His eyes were quick and scared. There was a lake of slick brown blood on the floor and a terrible stink they'd never be able to scrub out. At the hospital they said it was cancer, a big one impossible to get at. They gave him sleeping pills and morphine and said it was only a matter of a few days now. A bunch of us would go up and visit with him. He'd forget who you were and once began to call himself Robert Dickinson. "I don't know this Moley Gleeson. In the hospital with cancer? That's too bad. That's a real shame." It was as if his mind were trading places with someone named Robert Dickinson and in that way freeing itself from the bad business of being Moley Gleeson. We figured it was the drugs that were doing this to him.

We went over to Louis's house and asked him if there was anything he could do for Moley. We didn't think there was, seeing as how the doctors themselves said that his cancer was out of reach, but Louis dipped into his big doeskin medicine bag, took out some fine orange, brown, and green powders, and went into the bathroom with them. When he came out, he said, "Let's go see Moley."

The nurse who brought us to Moley's room wasn't too happy to see us again. "Now don't you boys tire out Mr. Gleeson. He's got about as much strength as a squashed cat." Louis closed the door behind us and tried to lock it but there was no way to do that from the inside. There were four or five of us in the room with him. Louis went to the window and looked skeptically at the light coming in. He adjusted the blinds, dimming the air. Moley was lying there, half-asleep. His eyes, when they opened, were covered with that glazed look of fear and loneliness the dying usually have. Louis looked at us with a strange expression in his eyes, as if we were familiar and new to him at the same time. We didn't know what to make of it, and so we kept ourselves at a respectable distance, figuring it was his show anyway. He bent his big shaggy head down to Moley and whispered something into his ear. We couldn't make out what it was but it took a long time, like a priest's last rites, so it was probably more than just "How ya doing, Moley?"

Louis pulled the sheet off Moley and then opened up his hospital gown. Moley looked like hell. There were bruises up and down his side and his arms were swollen up from the injections. His skin was soft and mushy-looking. He looked like a big wingless moth. He looked like he would come apart in your hands if you tugged at him. Louis rolled up his sleeves. He began to open and close his hands. His eyes were shut tight. Then he opened his hands wide. His hands began to stretch and taper out. They became long and narrow as snakes. They started to move toward Moley's underbelly and when they reached the pasty-white skin they didn't stop. His hands slid *into* Moley. Past the wrists. Up to the forearms. Moley's eyes were popped wide now, his mouth was ajar. I could see his tongue clicking around in there. Out of his mouth, from deep inside, I could hear a clacking, hammering sound, like wood on stone. The sweat was boiling out of Louis's forehead. He was searching around for something inside Moley, the way you'd feel the bottom of a swampy slough for something you'd dropped there. Then all at once the nurse comes busting into the room. She saw what was going on and began to holler for help. Louis was dragging something up. His forearms were dark red and the room smelled—a thin, sharp smell like arsenic smoke, comparable to what you'd expect just downwind of a smelter. What's coming out of Moley looks like an oblong head of lettuce. It's dark purple, nearly black, and wriggling like a speared eel. It was coming out of Moley's belly, just at the left of his navel and under the heart. If the thing had a head, then what I saw in it might have been eyes—dull and ugly, three of them in a row, looking around at the world of hospital rooms. The hammering sound that was coming out of Moley's throat had quit and Moley was grunting low and strong, with a kind of hard pleasure, like a woman giving easy birth.

A doctor came into the room. He hollered at Louis and then grabbed him by the beard. Another doctor came in and began to punch Louis in the back. But Louis hung on to the black lettuce eel, which, by the looks of it, was halfway out. The doctors were grinding their teeth and spitting curses at Louis and the nurse was running in and out of the room screaming for the cops. A young intern came in then with a steel chair in his hands. "Leave it to the Marines," he said. He took a baseball swing at Louis's head that landed with a gong. Louis staggered away from the blow but he didn't let loose of the thing in Moley's belly. The young intern swung the chair again and this time it dropped Louis to one knee. He lost his grip on the lettuce eel and it slipped back with a dark murmur into Moley to clack away at whatever was left of his innards. Moley sighed and went back to sleep, calling himself Robert Dickinson and telling us it was too bad about that poor bastard Moley Gleeson, whoever the hell he was. There was no mark or anything unusual at all on his belly. The blubbering nurse closed up Moley's gown and pulled his sheet up to his chin and Moley, a kind of dying amusement in his old black eyes, caught her trembling hands to steady her.

The police came in then and carried Louis off to jail. Three days later, Moley died.

Any prosecutor in the state would have had a hard time convincing a jury to lock up Louis Quenon because he had entered the insides of a dying man with his bare hands in order to prowl around in there for dangerous lettuce eels, and so, after holding Louis for a while, they decided to let him go, fining him twenty dollars for disorderly conduct.

They say that while he was in the pokey, Louis cured the police chief's wife of her insomnia by having the chief cut the ears off a live wild rabbit and strap them, still warm, to her temples before turning in at night. They say it cured more than her insomnia, though, and she began to want more in bed than her husband, who was almost sixty years old, could deliver. This made the chief think poorly of Louis and the word was put out that Louis had better keep his nose clean while in the city limits.

Louis got the blues after that episode. He'd come into Lucky's, but his smile was thin and far away and not meant for any of us who sat at his table. He didn't have any new stories to tell. We went ahead and asked him, "What's troubling you, Louis?" He'd take a deep lungful of air and let it sigh out. "You don't seem like yourself, Louis." He'd shake his head as if to unseat a fly and raise his beer to his lips. "Does it have to do with Moley?" we asked. "Or being in jail? Are you worried about the chief?" But he'd just look puzzled as if he didn't have the first idea of what we were talking about. Finally, after about a week of this, he said, "Step away." We did what he wanted because of our respect for him and no one tried to figure out why he said it.

It was about this time that Louis took a sales job with a farm implement company. Louis was well liked by the business people and could get work whenever he wanted it. Most people in the selling business knew that Louis had the power to move merchandise. They'd put him on straight commissions and he'd earn enough in three or four months to last him and Lily the year. I saw him one hot July afternoon driving a big green Farmall down the middle of the main drag leading a parade. He was wearing a wide-brim straw hat and sunglasses and I could tell by his color that he'd been drinking for a while. There was a troop of horsemen behind him, and behind them there was the high school marching band. A small crowd had gathered along the sidewalks to watch the parade, which was being held to celebrate the invention of the internal combustion engine. Behind the high school band there was a float that was supposed to illustrate the theme of the parade. It was a ten-foot-tall piston made out of silvered cardboard. Two girls in bathing suits were cranking the piston up and down. A three-year-old boy on top was dressed up like a spark plug. I saw Lily, narrower than ever, in the crowd of onlookers. She was walking slowly, so as to not get ahead of Louis's tractor. Her face was as colorless as skim milk. She was carrying her big red purse, but she wasn't holding it like a weapon. I could see by the look in her eyes that she was worried. I knew Lily didn't have any use for me or for any of us from Lucky's, but I caught up with her and touched her elbow anyway. "All of us over at Lucky's are pretty worried about Louis," I said.

"You have reason to be," she said, without taking offense or getting that look of total disgust she reserved for Louis's friends.

"What's troubling him, Mrs. Quenon?" I asked.

She looked at me then and the old contempt came back into her eyes for a second. "Dreams," she said.

She told me that Louis was having dreams he couldn't figure out. They'd started up when he was in jail and they got worse after they let him out. The dreams didn't scare him any, but he was having trouble reading them. He wrote to a man in Morocco, but all his letters had been returned unopened. Every night for a week he'd called an old friend of his named Art One Pipe who lived in the far northeast corner of the state. One Pipe told Louis that he was well known for his patience and not to act like a teenage girl with acne when he needed his best quality most. One Pipe drove the three hundred miles to see him and to help him work things out. "All they did was drink bourbon and puke," Lily said.

The word began to go around that Louis was in a bad way.

He'd quit his job after he'd made a couple of thousand dollars and had gone on a two-week tear, dropping most of it. Those of us who understood that Louis was the indispensable center of our circle as well as the spokes of the wheel that held it together, decided that something had to be done. I was elected to go to his house and make a plea, reminding him how important every one of us felt him to be. Lily let me in. She had an abandoned look on her face as if she didn't care what might happen next because the worst had already come about.

I found Louis in bed with a bottle of Canadian whiskey. He was naked and covered with a sheet. The room smelled fiercely of the rancid oil only a sick body can produce. He saw me and smiled a little. He tried to sit up. I helped him and fixed the pillows behind his head. He took the bottle of whiskey by the neck and poured some of it into his glass. He handed me the glass and took a drink himself directly out of the bottle. He had that same faraway look. I started to say something because I felt the time had come for me to say what I had come here to say, but he held up his hand to stop me. "Step away," he said.

I sat there for a full minute, not knowing what to do. Then I finished my drink and stood up. "Okay, Louis," I said. "But I'll come back a little later on, if that's all right with you."

Louis shook his head, frowning at my failure to understand him. "Me, I mean," he said. "*I'm* a step away. I think I always have been."

I guess I just had a blank look on my face. It seemed to exasperate him.

"The farther upstream you go," he said, slowly, as if he didn't trust my ability to understand simple English, "the meaner becomes the terrain. I'm tangled up in some high brush country, and it's beginning to look like there's a real chance I won't be able to go any farther or even find my way back."

"Uh-huh," I said.

"Sometimes these dreams say, 'Yes.' Sometimes they say, 'No.' Sometimes they say, 'You are ninety percent stone, and should spend the rest of your time selling tractors and making Lily happy and quit tampering with what you are not going to be able to figure out.' " He grunted at the humor of such a possibility.

"Do they ever tell you to go down to the yards and lay your head on a rail?" I mumbled into my empty glass.

Louis looked at me, his eyes sharp and mean. He hadn't had his hair cut for some time and it hung down over his ears, damp and oily-looking. He scratched his beard and chest. Then he grinned. I could see that his gums were nearly white and his teeth looked bad, too. "Maybe so," he said. Then he threw off his sheet and swung out of bed. "Hell," he said. "Let's go down to that place on the corner and hear some music."

That place on the corner, the closest bar to Louis's house, was a mean little cowboy bar called The Bar-None. The Bar-None was a long, narrow hole-in-the-wall with no elbowroom, no light, and no way to keep out of trouble. I thought it was the poorest idea Louis could have come up with but decided to string along, hoping that maybe we wouldn't get that far. Louis had to walk slow, with me holding his arm, because he'd been lying in bed for nearly a week with nothing but whiskey for food and feeling bad about everything. But by the time we got to The Bar-None, the fresh air and exercise had perked him up. "Why don't we go on down to Lucky's?" I suggested. It was only another four blocks.

"No," he said. "Too far. Too many leeches."

I can only say that I was knocked flat. It was the first truly unkind words I'd ever heard from Louis Quenon. I looked at him and he didn't try to avoid my eyes, but there was still too much distance in his face for it to mean anything to me.

We went in. There was the usual crowd of rough trade you never see anywhere except in places like The Bar-None. We took two stools toward the dark end of the bar. The jukebox was turned up loud and thumping. The lights were flickering—bad wiring. A fight was getting under way someplace in back. Louis ordered the first round of drinks. The cowboy next to me knocked my arm off the bar with his elbow. He didn't say he was sorry. He looked at me and then at Louis and then went on with his conversation. He was talking in an enterprising way to a nearly unconscious hawklike woman. A bloody face pushed itself between me and Louis and whispered hoarsely for a bottle of gin to go. Someone was trying to waltz with an Indian woman who hated the idea. She had dropped something on the floor but the hardleg she was with wouldn't let her stop long enough to pick it up. I decided to keep my eyes on the few square inches of bar in front of me until Louis figured he'd had enough of this place.

Someone came in by mistake. It was a woman and her husband. They had a dog on a leash. They stood in the doorway, squinting through the smoke haze and hammering roar. The woman said something to the man and they turned to leave. Something stopped them. Their dog, a gray poodle with a red ribbon on its neck, had gotten loose. Someone had scooped it up and set it on the bar. It skittered along, dodging glasses and hands, looking for a place to get down. The woman was trying to make her way toward it. "Banjo!" she yelled. "Banjo!" And pretty soon everyone in the place was yelling, "Banjo! Banjo!" and laughing crazy. Banjo was trembling and even though you could tell he didn't want to antagonize anyone, his lips began to curl back over his teeth in spite of himself, and he growled. This made everybody at the bar laugh all the harder. A cowboy with a long mortician's face stuck a Polish sausage into Banjo's mouth. The bartender snapped the bar rag at him and said, "Off, mutt." The strain was too much for Banjo. He peed. The pee rolled down against the face of a garage mechanic who had passed out on the bar. The woman next to the passed-out garage mechanic woke him up by tickling his throat with her fingernail. "You're laying in a puddle of poodle piss," she said, straight-faced. Those at the bar who heard it passed it down. "He's laying in a puddle of poodle piss," they said. Pretty soon nearly everyone in the place was saying it. For a minute there you couldn't hear yourself think. The garage mechanic began to realize that he was the butt of a joke of some kind. He wiped his face on his sleeve and looked at the trembling dog. He took the Polish sausage out of its mouth. Banjo tried to bark but only managed a humiliating whine. The mechanic grabbed the dog's leash and jerked it up into the air. The woman who had been trying to retrieve her dog broke into tears. She made a kind of high-pitched yelping sound that cut through the general racket. The mechanic held the dog over the bar by its leash. He looked at it as you might look at a wriggling fish on a line, trying to decide if it's a keeper or not. The dog's hind legs were digging frantically at the air. Then the mechanic began to twirl the dog in big lazy circles, letting the leash out to its full length. Everybody near them had to duck as the dog went by. The woman who owned the dog was screaming, "No! No! Please!" Her husband was still in the doorway, his hand on his forehead. Someone had put a country tune on the jukebox about a man and his hound. "Me and my hound, we go round and around." The woman had made her way to the mechanic. She began to punch him in the face. She didn't know how to punch, though. It looked like she was knocking at a door shyly, hoping that no one was home. The mechanic laughed and twirled the dog all the harder. Then his face went vicious and he gave the leash one more hard swing and let it go. The dog helicoptered through the air and landed somewhere in the dark rear of the bar. The woman was still putting her balled-up little fists in the mechanic's face. He grabbed her by the coat and lifted her off the floor. Then he set her down on the bar. Someone handed her a glass of beer. Her husband was still in the doorway, his hand on his forehead.

Louis sat through it all as if it were a partway interesting movie he was watching on the TV set above the bar. He took his whiskey neat and sipped it. Someone said, "This dog here is suffering." An old cowboy with the face of a child had picked up Banjo. The dog was having a convulsion. Louis slipped off his stool and went over to the old cowboy. "Look here," said the cowboy. "He needs a vet, real quick."

Louis took the dog from the arms of the old cowboy. He brought it over to the bar and laid it down on its side. He felt along the dog's spine and the back of its neck. He ran his fingers along the rib cage. The dog was jerking and its hind legs were trying to get traction. Louis opened the dog's jaws and put his fingers into its throat. The woman, who was still sitting on the bar holding the glass of beer they gave her, yelled, "What is he doing! What are his qualifications!" Her husband was still in the doorway. He raised his hand as if to get someone's permission to speak. Louis pressed his ear against the dog. He straightened up then and looked at the woman down the bar.

"Your doggie is dead, ma'am," he said.

She heard him. "No!" she yelled. "Look, he's still moving his legs! Here, Banjo! Here, my darling!"

Louis pushed the dog aside to the man next to him and he in turn pushed it aside, and so on, until the dog finally got to the woman. She picked it up and held it close to her face. She began to speak to it in baby talk. Banjo began to wag his tail.

"No use," Louis said. "That dog is dead."

Banjo got to his feet and began to dance up and down, trying to lick the woman's tear-streaked face. A man and a woman were trading Sunday punches next to the men's room. The woman would take a punch, then grin and spit at the man. Then the man would take a punch from the woman and he would also grin and spit. It was some sort of contest. They were both heavyweights, two hundred pounds or more.

"No use," Louis said again. "No use in carrying on like that. The doggie is dead."

The garage mechanic helped the woman down from the bar and she and her poodle made their way back to the man in the doorway. The little dog was barking happily and jumping up and down against the woman's legs.

"It's dead," Louis said. "They shouldn't fool themselves like that. It only makes it harder."

Louis left town for a couple of months. No one knew where he went. When he came back, Art One Pipe was with him. One Pipe had brought most of his belongings. Louis put him up in a spare room. Lily, by that time, had had enough. One Pipe was the last straw, and she moved out, taking a room in the George A. Custer Hotel, uptown.

Louis had changed. He'd lost a lot of weight and he looked ten years older. I never realized how tall he was. When he was filled out, you didn't notice his height so much. But now he was skin on bone and had taken off his beard. His hair was cropped short. We'd see him, now and then, walking uptown, his clothes flapping on him like there wasn't anything inside them. His big round face looked sunken in and his shoulder blades poked up against his shirt like broken-off wings. He must have been close to seven feet tall and it looked as though he had all he could do just to keep standing upright, like a narrow reed that had outgrown its ability to keep itself straight. He never came into Lucky's and those of us who once counted on his being around gave him up for lost. No one came right out and said it, but it was in the air every time two or more of us would sit down together. Then the stories began to come in.

Louis had begun to stop people in the street to tell them what they didn't want to hear. He would block their way and point a finger in their faces, like a crazy prophet, drunk on his own visions. "Your baby will likely be torn up pretty bad in a baler," he told a woman, who fainted dead away on the spot. "The day after you have the family photograph taken, happiness will fly out of your window forever," he told a young pair of newlyweds. "In the little sealed-off rooms behind your eyes there is a coiled-up animal itching to drill holes in your ability to figure things out," he said to Nestor Claig, the high school principal and supposedly the smartest man in town. Sometimes he'd act as if he were listening to people's deepest thoughts. He'd cock an ear at them, squint, then put his big hand on their shoulders. "No, never do that twice," he whispered into the long hair of a beautiful young woman. "The corrected promise is all you can hope for," he said to a tired-looking man of fifty. And to a bank vice president, he said, "Her mind, you know, is shot through with tidy lies. Leave her before she drags you under."

Someone called the police and they threatened to lock him up again for disturbing the peace. The chief went to Lily with a plan to have Louis put away in the state mental hospital. But Lily didn't want any part of the chief's plan. "He keeps this up, Lily," said the chief, "and we won't need you to sign any papers. I'll get the court to put him away."

"Do what you want," Lily said. "Just don't ask me to do your job for you."

Then one day Lily showed up at Lucky's with a gentleman friend.

He was over seventy and wore a fine silk suit. He carried a black cane and had a little white mustache. Lily had a proud look on her face. Her eyes dared anyone to say something. No one paid them any attention except when they moved their hands or opened their mouths to speak. Lily didn't care. She talked in a loud, relaxed voice about the big savings-and-loan company her gentleman friend used to work for as chief accountant. He didn't seem to mind her bragging him up. He'd sit with one hand in his lap and his other hand on a glass of sweet port, a real gentleman. He had a calm, distant gaze on his face that seemed to reach all the way back to Minneapolis, where he'd spent his best years. His name was Roland Towne. He lived in the room across from Lily's in the George A. Custer.

This went on for a while. Then Louis caught sight of them together, on the sidewalk, heading for Lucky's. He trailed them to the door but he didn't follow them inside. We could see him in the doorway, silhouetted against the light, like a staring pile of bones. Lily ignored him. Roland Towne ignored everything. Leonard would get a worried look on his face every time Lily and Roland came in trailed by Louis. "This is coming to a head," he whispered to me.

He was right. You could see that Louis was becoming agitated. He began to pace up and down in front of Lucky's, biting his fingernails and scratching his beard, which he'd begun to let grow again. He was still skinny, though, as if he'd given up the idea of eating proper food. One evening he came into Lucky's with Art One Pipe. Lily and Roland weren't there. "I'm going to tell you people something you probably don't want to hear," he said, to all of us. Art One Pipe shook his head. "Hell, Louis," he said. "It's better you just kept quiet."

Louis ignored him. "I was in the Badlands. Don't ask *me* how I got there. It was a dream. There had been a terrible drought. I hadn't sold a tractor in over a month. A custom cutting crew brought their combines in from Kansas, took one look at the dead, empty land, and got mean drunk for a week. And then, all at once, I was up north, in the Badlands, alone. What am I doing here? I said to myself. I met a woman who called herself Mrs. Tree. She was big and fat. She didn't know what I was doing there either.

She lived in a mud-wall cabin. She said that she was responsible for the weather. She'd been sick. The wind had blown something bad into her ear. She couldn't remember things. Like the patterns of her stones. She had to line up some stones, big round ones that she had to shove with her shoulder. Every day she had to line them up in a different pattern just so the weather would stay normal. But the bad thing that had been blown into her ear made her forget the patterns."

Louis took a swallow of beer. One Pipe was staring into his whiskey glass. He had a slightly disgusted look on his face. Louis paid him no attention. "So I told her," Louis continued. "I said, 'I can fix up your memory with a little bit of this tea here.' I made her some and she drank it down. Her eyes lit up. 'That's real good,' she said. 'I almost remember everything now.' 'Almost?' I said. 'There is one more thing,' she said. She took off her dress and laid down in the dirt. 'You have got to be my husband for a little while.' There was a dangerous look in her black eyes but at the moment she only seemed flirtatious and coy to me. So I piled on her and we were getting to it before long like a husband and wife."

"Take it easy, Louis," Leonard said. "There's mixed company here."

"Filthy lunatic," said an elderly prim woman in a flaming red wig.

Louis ignored these protests. "But just as I reached the point of no return, I felt myself starting to shrink. At the same time, I got groggy and weak. Something was pulling me in, a powerful suction that had started to fold me in half, backward, at the hips. I mean to tell you that it came from *her,* that I was being sucked up into *her,* like the reverse of being born. Everything went black and warm and I could hear her heart thudding over me someplace like a rhythmic thunder. I moved upward, sort of swimming, sort of flying, in the pitch-black dark. Then there was something in front of me. A big, hard-shelled bug of some kind, like a sow bug, only it was half as big as me. It blocked my path. 'Kill it,' said Mrs. Tree. I was real surprised that I was able to hear her voice. It was like she was behind me someplace, talking through a culvert. I picked the sow bug up in my hands and killed it easy enough, but it took a while and it stank something terrible. Then I felt myself falling. Down down down I went until I hit something soft and warm. Pressure like I never felt before pressed me from all sides. I was being squeezed down smaller and smaller. I wanted to cry out but there was no air to be had. Then the light hit me again like the blast of an atomic bomb. I was out in the open air flat on the mud floor of her hut, covered with blood and crying. She had given birth to me. I was her baby."

"Will someone please call the police?" said the prim woman in the red wig.

"When I was myself again," Louis said, unbothered by the interruption, "Mrs. Tree said, 'Thank you. You killed the thing that had gotten into my ear. I feel a lot better. I remember everything now.' We crossed over to where her stones were kept and she shoved them around with her shoulders until they formed a pattern of X's, circles, and stars. It was a lot of hard work and it took a long time. When she was done, she went into her mud hut and laid down to sleep. Pretty soon a big black cloud comes boiling out of Canada. 'Going to hail,' I said. Mrs. Tree pokes her head out of her hut and gives me a funny look. 'Be quiet, you,' she said. 'I got to sleep. The weather is back to normal now.' And sure enough, the white stuff starts jumping all around us, hail, big and lumpy. But something's wrong with it. It isn't exactly hail. After it hits the ground, it moves around and tries to sit up. I bend down to get a closer look. It's the figure of a man. Millions of them. They are all pasty white and naked as day one. They can't be alive, but they are. Half-alive anyway, and cold to the touch, cold as the hail I thought they were. You'd pick one of them up in your hand and he'd turn over and look at you with those sad icy-white eyes. There was no real energy in them. They seemed to be carved out of soft white soap. They didn't have any mouths to speak of, and they didn't have any assholes. You can't get the medicine into them and you can't get the poison out. They would just turn over and look at you with those miserable dead-cold icy-white eyes. They had little frosty mustaches and each one of them was holding on to a little glass of that sweet port. They made you want to puke. All they can do is think about how it used to be back in Minneapolis a hundred and ten years ago. I hollered into Mrs. Tree's hut that it would be better to have the drought, but it was too late, she was dead to the world of ordinary people."

He told this story as a daily routine. The details of Louis's dream would change, but it always ended with the little ice-cold men falling out of the cloud. I believed it was a real dream and that he'd just doctored it up a little so that it seemed to be especially about Roland Towne. Then one day, he told it while Lily and Roland were in the bar. Leonard looked like he expected trouble. The rest of us went on with business as usual. When Louis finished with the story, he stared directly at Roland. Roland nodded to him, amiable, and took a sip of his port. Lily was red as a turnip, having been insulted by the off-color dream and its outrageous ending. She had her big red purse with her, ready for action.

Louis had something with him. It was a moth-eaten blanket with wheels and thunderbirds stitched on it. He walked over to the table where Lily and Roland were sitting. He took something out of a pouch he was carrying and sprinkled it in the air over Roland's head. Then he unfolded the blanket and tossed it on top of Roland so that the old man was completely covered by it. Lily's jaw dropped. She gave Louis a thud on the back with her purse. Louis mumbled a little hocus-pocus in a foreign language. Roland didn't move. You could see his outline under the blanket. He was a cool old man. He let Louis ramble on. I saw the shape of his glass slide up the blanket as he raised it to his lips and then back down as he returned it to the table. He was drinking his sweet port as if nothing at all peculiar was happening. Louis took the blanket off with a big swooping yank. Roland's white hair was mussed a little and there was a scattering of green dust in it, but other than that he looked serene as ever if not slightly bored. He nodded to Louis, still amiable, and took another sip of his wine, his mind nine hundred and fifty miles dead east. Some people are like that. Something inside of them is solid as rock even though their exteriors seem frail and delicate. I had to give old Roland credit. Louis gave him too much credit, though. He stumbled backward, swallowing hard, as if Roland had leveled a Smith & Wesson .38 at his nose. I don't know for sure, but I think Louis had tried to make the old accountant disappear. It didn't work.

Louis got desperate after that. He got an old Model T ignition coil from the junkyard and began to give himself strong electrical shocks with Art One Pipe's reluctant help. These shocks were supposed to rejuvenate something that had gone dormant inside of him. When winter came, he stood for an hour in a blizzard without any clothes on, singing magical songs into the north wind. In the spring, he went on a diet of berries, bark, and roots. He slept in the skin of a grizzly killed eighty years ago by an Indian's arrow. The Indian had broken some kind of spiritual law by killing the grizzly and the skin was said to be inhabited by an angry spirit. Louis wanted to strike a deal with this dark spirit.

The dreams he had while sleeping in that skin led him to do things to himself that were painful and dangerous. He stuck long pins into his feet. He swallowed ordinary garden dirt, worms and all. He nearly blinded himself in the left eye with some kind of caustic. He dunked himself into the June rapids of the Sweetroot River and was swept downstream a mile before he could beach himself.

He learned new songs and sayings all the way from Alaska. He made a telephone call to North Africa and talked for an hour to a hostile bureaucrat who wouldn't give him the information he wanted. He rode freight trains to the West Coast and drank saltwater out of the Pacific Ocean where two great currents met in a war of waves, and when he came back he set fire to everything he owned except his medicine bag and his house.

He was thrown in jail again, let out, thrown back in again, forced to spend a couple of months in the state mental hospital, let out, and so on, in a battle between the authorities and Louis's ever-widening circle of desperate actions.

The town formed a committee to deal with the problem. He visited the committee meetings in white skins and paint on his face. He would sit in the back row, by himself, staring at the members of the committee without comment. One by one the committee members found strange-looking figures carved out of wood stuck into their front lawns. The chairman of the committee found a necklace of dead mice hung on his mailbox. But the committee members, all hardheaded businessmen, scoffed at Louis's mumbo-jumbo. Once Louis brought his moth-eaten blanket to the committee meeting, threw some of that green dust into the air, sang something in a falsetto voice, waved the blanket, but if it was meant to make the committee disappear into thin air, it didn't work. A couple of the members, though, came down with the flu shortly after that.

Art One Pipe had long since gotten fed up with Louis and had left town. Lily filed for a divorce. She got it quick and without any catches. She married Roland Towne a few days later and they went back to Minneapolis, forever.

Louis moved into an old mineshaft on a hill just south of town and was rarely seen anymore. People began to think of him as a harmless old hermit. They liked it that way. So long as he stayed up in his cave brooding, everybody was happy. Everybody got the idea that Louis had found his proper place in the world. "That crazy old hermit" is what you'd hear, always said with a kind of relief. And then all the old stories would take on a comic element. There had always been something awe-inspiring about Louis, but now people would chuckle and shake their heads remembering the funny side of his antics. Only a few of us remembered how it really was. Even some who had been given a cure for one thing or another would now tell you how most disease was really ninety percent in your head, anyway. "One cure is as good as the next if you believe in it, for the mind is the true healer." Or, put another way: "If you think you're sick, then by God you *are* sick, or soon will be." One old fool who Louis had raised up out of a hospital bed argued, "It wasn't my heart that was bad, it was my *attitude*." A husband who had promised to give Louis a two-year-old Cadillac if he could help his wife said, "Hell, she wore that cancer like a glove. When she decided to take it off because she wasn't getting any *mile*age off it anymore, off it *came*." Louis got the Cadillac, but it had piston slap and the transmission was balky.

After hearing this sort of talk one afternoon in Lucky's, I jumped up and yelled, "You're all ingrates and liars!" I danced a little old man's war dance, holding a chair out in front of me like a weapon or a dance partner. "Look at me!" I said. "I had one foot in the grave all the way up to the hip before Louis came along!"

But no one pays much attention to a white-haired seventy-year-old man doing a war dance with a chair. A few of them chuckled and Leonard turned up the TV so that the baseball game would drown out my little commotion. An Indian woman named Nan Person came over to my table and sat down. She was about sixty years old, tall and angular. She had a fine long jaw but not many teeth in it. Her leathery hands were beautiful—slender and calm.

"They only feel betrayed," she said.

"What?" I was still a little hot. I stared at her and she didn't look away. "You don't make sense," I said.

"They are mad at him for going crazy," she said. "They feel like fools, having put their faith in a crazy man. Now they are proving to themselves that nothing ever happened to them."

That made me laugh. I touched Nan Person's hand. "One thing is sure," I said. "Nothing will ever happen to them again."

She laughed too, and I picked up her fine hand and kissed it.

But another thing did happen to them. It was a Sunday afternoon, maybe as much as a year later. A few of us were sitting around having some muscatel. Nan Person, who had moved in with me, was holding my hand under the table. A love affair so late in life is an undreamed-of thing. But there it was, full-blown and real. A gift from nowhere for no good reason, but taken with gratitude and no questions asked. We never discussed it, Nan and me. It was there, in our eyes, a crazy thing that made us sweet and giddy.

Something was in the air that day. I saw Nan shiver slightly, with that nervousness you feel before an important event. It was quiet. The quiet was inside of you and outside of you. I didn't know I was holding my breath until I got dizzy. A few others were glancing at the doors every now and then. Leonard was sitting at the end of the bar where he kept the 12-gauge shotgun, pretending to read the newspaper. The TV set was on. A bullnecked preacher was hollering to beat hell into ten microphones. The sound was turned off, but the address of where you could send your money was being flashed across the bottom of the screen. Bullneck wasn't taking any chances.

I excused myself from the table to get a little air. The street was empty. It had rained hard earlier that day and everything was still wet and clean-looking. I was thinking how fine and permanent everything is in spite of all the individual comings and goings and the hoopla that goes with it, when a big hand touched me on the shoulder. It was Louis.

"Must have been the Apple of Peru," he said, as if resuming a conversation we might have been having two or three years ago. I looked at him. He looked good. He was filled out and he had gotten himself a clean suit of ordinary clothes that almost fit. His hair was plastered down and his beard had been combed. My eyes must have been watery because he also seemed blurred around the edges, like an old photo that had seen too much sunlight. "Also known," he went on, "as the angel's trumpet, stinkweed, nightshade, and Jamestown weed. You may have heard the bastardized version, which is most popular in this neck of the woods. Jimson weed. That's what it must have been."

I figured he meant for me to ask him what he was talking about, so I did.

"I grew some," he said, "up on that hill, among a lot of other things. I sang a number of serious lamentations, and I needed helpers. But living up there in that mineshaft aggravated my piles, and my gonads had begun to produce severe and regular aches. Apple of Peru is a good helper for such troubles."

I wiped the blur out of my eyes. He came into focus for a second; then his edges got threadbare again. "Have you come back down?" I asked.

He didn't say anything. He stroked his beard and looked up and down the street as if it were the first time he'd been on it. He seemed to be vibrating like a tuning fork. I don't mean he was trembling as if he had the shakes after a killer binge. I just mean you couldn't concentrate on his *edges*. "Let's go have a drink," he said. "I'll tell you about it."

There was a general shamefaced welcoming commotion inside.

Tables were shoved together and pitchers of beer were ordered. Leonard brought over a fresh bottle of Louis's favorite whiskey. Louis poured himself a generous shot. He stared at the glass for a minute. We waited. Then he pushed it slowly away. "I'd better not," he said, and everyone murmured something in an understanding way, since it was pretty clear that Louis had been dry for quite a while.

"Apple of Peru," he said. "That, and the fact that there's a big deposit of pitchblende in that hill. It wasn't hard to figure out what happened. At first, anyway. Then . . ."

You could hear everyone suck air as Louis picked up the shot glass and sipped at it. "What the hell," he said. "Spirits for the spirit, what's the harm?"

We didn't ask him what he was talking about. But Nan heard something in his tone of voice, a change, that made her dig her long, slender fingers into my leg. She leaned on me and her lanky body suddenly felt frail.

"Apple of Peru," Louis said again. "It has a characteristic way of getting down into your marrow. It probably had some pitchblende in it, too. I got real sick. But I got . . . *healthy,* too. Healthy in a way I'd never been."

He looked *too* tall all of a sudden. It was as if he were sitting on a pillow, giving him a few extra inches of height. A humming swarm of small white moths flew out of his left ear. I blinked and looked around to see if anyone else had seen them, but no one looked amazed. I took a long drink of wine.

"Leeches," Louis said, looking directly at me. He was smiling a little, as though we were sharing a private joke. A few people took offense at the remark and left the table, but they were the ones who had scoffed loudest at the memory of Louis's cures.

"Fever moved into me like a weather front," Louis said, resuming his story. "I went into a coma, I think. I was way back in that mineshaft, wrapped in a tarp. I think I was unconscious for two or three days. It's dark way back in a stope, darker than any night in the woods, and when I woke up . . . I could see a glow. It was coming from me, from my bones, from my blood, greenish-white, like I'd swallowed a quart of radium."

A round of throat clearing passed through Lucky's. No one was willing to swallow this part of his story. Some chair legs scraped the floor as the doubters got ready to depart.

"I was crazy for a while. I would run around the hillside, hollering and throwing myself down, flailing and kicking at imaginary beings. You could probably hear me all the way in town on a clear night. Once I tried to bite the moon, which had hooked itself onto my shoulder like a big cocklebur. It was trying to turn itself into a pair of wings. Owl wings. These were dreams and they were not dreams."

Louis got up and went to the front windows of the bar. He pulled down the shades. He then turned off the overhead lights. That made it pretty dark inside. At first you couldn't see anything except the blue glow of the TV set, where the bullneck preacher was now crying like a child, his thick, ham-pink face straining under a perfectly timed emotion, since the service was about over. He bit his lip and blinked back tears.

"I'm crouched down behind the bar, I think," Louis said. "Or maybe I'm behind the jukebox. I'll give your eyes another minute to get used to the dark, then I'll come out. Then you'll see what I'm talking about."

It was a long minute. The preacher had finished weeping and was now smiling up at the sky, where heavenly approval fell on him in the form of swiftly moving spotlights. Then someone slammed a glass down. I guess I was looking in the wrong place. I turned to the left and then to the right. Nan caught my face in her long hand and aimed it straight ahead.

The white moths I had seen swarming out of his ear had now formed themselves into the shape of a skeleton. The jaws of the skull opened. "Pitchblende," it said.

"Turn on the lights!" someone begged. A chair was knocked over. Someone bumped into someone else and cursed. Nan stood up, dragging me out of my chair. The glowing bones drifted toward us. But now their shape changed. They weren't bones piled on bones anymore. It was a circle of moths.

"I'm dreaming on my feet," Louis said, but his voice wasn't coming from anywhere near the moths.

Nan jerked me to one side as the moths came closer, but it was too late to avoid them. We were in them, passing through them. It was like passing through an electrical portal of some kind that took you from one place to another. I felt the hair on my head move.

Nan and I were running, hand in hand, over chairs and tables, over the bar, over brick walls and alleys and parked cars until we were nowhere near Lucky's or town but in a big, grassy, sunblown field, not scared but *eager,* not escaping but *finding.*

We were young. I saw how beautiful she had been, and I felt my own young strength as we loped across that meadow, kicking the heads off dandelions, the bees thick and busy, the cottonwoods at the meadow's end leaning pleasurefully against the perfumed breeze. "Keep going!" I yelled. "Don't stop!"

Leonard raised the shades and switched on the lights. I sipped my muscatel, Nan sipped hers. Louis raised his glass of whiskey and squinted at it. "Whew," he said softly.

"Louis," said some old man with rheumy eyes. "I got this numbness in my foot . . ."

"No more cures," Louis said. "The world has gone stale. Not the world of trees and rocks and animals, but the world that men have made. We hate it so bad we are itching to blow it up. I didn't go up on that mountain to figure out some new cures. It's useless to get rid of cancer in a man who can't tell the difference between the urge to grin and the urge to spit."

The baseball game came on and Leonard turned up the sound. Attention drifted gradually from Louis to the television set.

"Let's take a walk," Louis said to Nan and me. "There's more to tell."

Outside, Louis said in a dreamy way, "I was born with a caul, you know. My mother wouldn't have anything to do with me for a month. She figured it meant I could see and converse with ghosts. She was superstitious." He laughed. We laughed too, but we weren't too sure of what it was we found funny.

We walked up Main Street. The air was thin and cool for midsummer. Out of the corner of my eye I saw Nan shiver. I wondered if she had dreamed of a perfect meadow, felt her strong young legs pounding the grass as the pollen-heavy bees bounced off our bare arms.

"I'm not here," Louis said.

Nan grunted, as if her suspicions had been borne out.

"I'm in that shaft," Louis said. "I'm in that tarp. I could already be dead. Maybe dead for weeks."

Nan let some air hiss out between her teeth.

I felt light as a moonwalker. It seemed that I might float off if a good breeze came up. Some Sunday strollers were out. Louis nodded to them and they nodded back. Louis's nod seemed to say, Let's let bygones be bygones.

I was tingling all over. The atoms of my skin and the atoms of the air were mingling. The sidewalk felt like it was paved with marshmallow. Nan squeezed my arm until it hurt. She nodded at Louis, meaning for me to take a good look.

Although his edges were blurrier than ever, he looked good. I was proud, as I always had been, to be his friend. I was thinking, Isn't it nice that things never really end and what appears to be finished often fools you and more often than not comes back to start all over again with only minor changes for the sake of variety. Louis turned and smiled at me. It was a smile that could make you feel that you'd finally gotten the point after years and years of pretending there wasn't one.

We walked to the far end of Main Street, where the town ends. Then Nan and I, on our own now, turned and drifted slowly back.

RICK DEMARINIS is the author of six novels, including *The Year of the Zinc Penny*, which the *New York Times Book Review* cited as a notable work of fiction of 1989, and *The Burning Women of Far Cry*, and a previous story collection: *Under the Wheat*, winner of the Drue Heinz Literature Prize. His new story collection, *Voice of America*, has just been published by Norton. His stories have appeared in *Harper's, Antaeus, Story, Epoch, Cutbank*, and other periodicals. In 1990 he received a Literature Award from the American Academy and Institute of Arts and Letters. He teaches creative writing at the University of Texas, El Paso.